'So how did y

Alice laughed. 'I v
of all people wo
babies come from.'

Jeremy grinned, but pressed on unfazed. 'It's a natural question to ask. Was it planned?'

'That's none of your business,' Alice responded. 'You were the one who said I didn't have to reveal anything I didn't want to.'

'But that was to the patients,' Jeremy answered straightforwardly. 'I'm a friend.'

Alice looked at him. 'You're also my boss.'

Carol Marinelli did her nursing training in England and then worked for a number of years in Casualty. A holiday romance while backpacking led to her marriage and emigration to Australia. Eight years and three children later, the romance continues…

Today she considers both England and Australia her home. The sudden death of her father prompted a reappraisal of her life's goals and inspired her to tackle romance-writing seriously.

Recent titles by the same author:

THE EMERGENCY ASSIGNMENT
DR CARLISLE'S CHILD
THE OUTBACK NURSE

THE PREGNANT INTERN

BY
CAROL MARINELLI

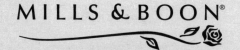

MILLS & BOON®

For Sam, Alex and Lucinda
with love.

All the characters in this book have no existence outside the imagination of the author, and have no relation whatsoever to anyone bearing the same name or names. They are not even distantly inspired by any individual known or unknown to the author, and all the incidents are pure invention.

*First published in Great Britain 2002
Harlequin Mills & Boon Limited,
Eton House, 18-24 Paradise Road, Richmond, Surrey TW9 1SR*

© Carol Marinelli 2002

ISBN 0 263 83069 1

*Set in Times Roman 10½ on 11½ pt.
03-0502-53036*

*Printed and bound in Spain
by Litografía Rosés, S.A., Barcelona*

PROLOGUE

'YOUR blood pressure's up.'

Alice let out the breath she had inadvertently been holding. She had been trying to keep her breathing even and think only pleasant thoughts as Brett Halliday, her obstetrician, checked her blood pressure, apparently to no avail.

'By very much?'

Brett shook his head as he unwrapped the cuff. 'Not much. It's just up a touch, and still within a safe margin, but still…' He sat down at his heavy wooden desk and leant across the table as Alice, avoiding his gaze and desperately trying to avoid the ensuing conversation, concentrated rather too intently on rolling down her sleeve.

'I've been rushing around this morning, and it's terribly hot. Anyway, you know how nervous I get at these antenatal appointments.'

Brett nodded. 'All of which I've taken into consideration, but it still doesn't alter the fact that your blood pressure is a little higher than I'd like it to be.' He flicked through the pile of pathology results in front of him.

'Your blood work all looks OK, though your haemoglobin level is only scraping into the normal limits range. You're still taking your iron tablets, I assume?'

Alice nodded.

'Well, try to increase your iron intake from natural means also. Lots of green leaf vegetables and iron-rich foods—and plenty of vitamin C,' he added. 'It helps with iron absorption. You know the routine.'

'But everything is all right with the baby?' she asked anxiously.

Brett gave her a reassuring smile. 'The baby's doing nicely—nice size, lots of movement. It's the mum I'm more worried about.'

'Honestly, Brett, I'm fine.' Her words came out rather too harshly. Alice could hear the anxiety in her own voice and paused for a second to regain control. It was imperative to have Brett Halliday onside. With a stroke of his expensive fountain pen he could sign her off work and that was absolutely the last thing she needed at the moment. 'Really, I'm fine,' Alice said, more evenly, even managing a small smile.

But she wasn't going to escape a lecture. 'Look, Alice, you're twenty-five weeks now. Most women at this stage are starting to wind down and looking forward to their maternity leave, not about to commence a three-month surgical internship at a busy city hospital. You don't need me to tell you how busy Melbourne City is—you've spent the last nine months there for yourself. And Jeremy Foster may be a fine surgeon, but he's coming back from a long stint on sick leave. He's going to have a large backlog to catch up on and, more to the point, a lot to prove.'

'What do you mean?' Alice asked, her curiosity about her new boss for a moment overriding the issue of whether or not she worked.

'Well, it was a serious motor crash he was in. No one really expected him to live, let alone walk. And now here he is, less than a year later, returning to work, apparently none the worse for wear. There's going to be people watching him—rightly or wrongly, he's going to have to do a lot of spadework to convince them he's up to the job.'

'But he's a brilliant surgeon,' Alice argued defensively. She hadn't yet met Jeremy Foster, but you didn't have to meet Jeremy to feel as if you knew him. He had broken more hearts throughout the hospital than Alice could keep track of. But despite his somewhat scandalous reputation there had never been any question as to his surgical brilliance. 'He was the hospital's rising star—I'm lucky to have got a place on his team.'

'"Was" being the operative word. Look, Alice, Jeremy's going to be under the pump and that means more work for you.'

'I can handle it. Honestly, Brett, I'll be fine. This three-month stint will take me up to thirty-seven weeks. Lots of first babies come late, which will give me nearly a month to put my feet up and think baby thoughts. Heaps of women work practically until they go into labour these days.' She sounded so confident Alice almost convinced herself that she could handle it, but Brett wasn't about to be fobbed off.

'True,' he said, then added gently, 'But those women probably have a partner to come home to, or at least a supportive family. Someone to give them a bit of help and take away some of the strain. I know how much you need this, Alice, and I don't want to ruin your plans—but I have to be sure you know what you're doing.'

His words, however kindly meant, tore through her. The cool, confident façade melted in an instant and as she crumpled before him Brett came around the desk and handed her a handful of tissues.

'I'm sorry,' she sniffed. 'I didn't want to cry in front of you. In front of anyone,' she added.

'Cry away,' Brett said kindly. 'I see a lot of tears in here. You're not the only pregnant woman trying to make it all work. Trying to cram it all in before the baby comes along. Sometimes you need someone else to make the decision for you. To put the brakes on and tell you to slow down.'

Alice didn't answer. Accepting the tissues, she wept for a moment. She felt mortified that it had come to this: sitting in a doctor's office, begging to be allowed to work, begging for the chance to support her baby.

'If I don't finish my internship I won't be registered as a doctor and that means I can't apply to go on a GP training rotation.'

'But you can do your surgical internship once the baby comes along.'

Alice shook her head. 'I'm living in a bedsit. I can hardly afford the rent as it is. If I stop working—'

'You can claim child support,' Brett said in a practical voice. 'You won't starve.'

'I don't want my baby to start out life like that. You know how big the incentives are for country GPs. I'd have a home, a job. I could afford to have someone look after the baby while I work. I'd be able to give it a real future. If I don't do this it will put my plans back by months.'

'What about your parents? I know they're in Adelaide and you've had your differences, but maybe they're starting to get used to the idea now. Perhaps if you explained to your mum the problems that you're having, trying to make it all work…'

Her stricken look said it all. 'Then what about the baby's father?' Brett ventured gently. 'Shouldn't he be helping? After all, legally it *is* his responsibility.'

He watched as she stiffened. 'He wants nothing to do with me or the baby,' Alice said in a strained voice. 'He made that perfectly clear.'

'He might not want anything to do with you both,' Brett said, making his way back to his seat, 'but there are laws out there to protect women in exactly your position. Maybe it's time he faced up to the truth that he's about to become a father and the responsibility that entails. Even if it's only financially.'

For the first time Alice didn't have to pretend to be assured or confident; this was the one area of her life that was unequivocal. 'I'm not asking him for a single cent. He's either in or out of this baby's life—not somewhere in between. Marcus made it perfectly clear it was the latter he was choosing when I found out I was pregnant, and as far as I'm concerned it can stay that way. I want nothing more to do with him.

'Look, Brett, I really need this job,' she pleaded. 'If you think I'm stressed now, I'd be ten times worse if you told me I couldn't work. If there was any question that my baby was in danger, of course I wouldn't start, but you said yourself the baby's fine.'

Brett didn't answer for what seemed like an age. Instead, he started writing up her notes before finally looking up. 'All right, then. But I want to see you fortnightly from now on. And if your blood pressure creeps any higher, or I've even the slightest hint that either you or the baby aren't coping, I'll sign you off—and I mean it, Alice. Get yourself some support tights, eat the right food and put your feet up every chance you get.'

Alice grinned as she stood up. 'I promise.'

Brett found himself smiling back at her. He had been unsure there as to what to do. Instinct told him to sign her off, but he could understand her desperation. It was a tough call all right. Yet there was no doubt that Alice looked a lot more relaxed now she could go ahead with her plans. If he took her blood pressure now, he'd half expect it to be normal.

'Make an appointment with Madge on your way out. I do late nights on Mondays for my working mums—that'll probably suit you better.'

'Thanks.' Smiling, she made her way down the long carpeted corridor to the reception desk. 'It's OK, baby,' she whispered, gently patting her bump as she walked. 'Mummy's going to be able to take good care of you now. We're going to be just fine.'

CHAPTER ONE

WHOEVER had written in the mother-and-baby magazine Alice had read in the doctor's waiting room that there was a lot more choice in maternity wear these days either had a bottomless wallet or terrible taste in clothes, Alice thought ruefully as she dressed. Her 'bump' seemed to have grown practically overnight. Though somewhat excited by the rapid changes in her body, the down side was she could no longer get by with undoing the buttons of her skirts and wearing loose-fitting clothes. Her trip to the maternity departments hadn't been a howling success. Everything was either ludicrously expensive or trimmed with a disgusting lace Peter Pan collar or bow. Finally she had settled on a 'maternity kit' which consisted of a black Lycra skirt, swing top and trousers, and a little black dress which showed off rather a lot of her expanding bust line. Still, it was reasonably priced and, teamed with a couple of shirts, it should get her through the remainder of her pregnancy.

Settling on the black skirt and top, she pulled her dark hair back into a low ponytail and applied her make-up. The 'glow' the same magazine had promised would appear by mid-pregnancy seemed to be about as evasive as a black maternity bra. But with a touch of eyeliner and mascara on her long lashes, and a dash of lipstick on her full mouth, she didn't look too bad, Alice thought as she eyed herself in her bathroom mirror. Picking up her bag, she had a quick check in the full-length mirror and let out a groan. She looked as if she were going to a funeral. Despite the manufacturer's claims, there was obviously no such thing as 'sheer' forty denier support tights. 'You're going to be late on your first day,' Alice warned herself as she hastily ripped off the offending garment and grappled through her bathroom cabinet for some tinted moisturiser. She hadn't been near the beach in months and her pale legs needed a bit of help. Finally—if not entirely happy with her appearance, at least feeling marginally better—Alice took a tram the short distance to the hospital and amazingly arrived with ten minutes to spare.

'Morning. It's Alice Masters, isn't it?'

'That's right.' She smiled at the friendly freckled face. 'You must be Josh Winters, the surgical resident.'

'The one and only. Looks as if it's only us two here. Linda McFarlane's probably sucking a few lemons before the ward round.'

'I'm glad it's not just me who thinks like that. I had more than a few reservations when I first met her. She's not very friendly, is she?' Alice said, referring to the surgical registrar who had been particularly condescending at her interview.

'Tell me about it! Darren Barker, the other reg, is nice to work with but unfortunately he's on annual leave for a month now Jeremy's back. I wish it was Linda who was on leave—she told me to get a haircut before they'd consider me.'

'And did you?' Alice asked eyeing the long shaggy locks reaching well past his collar.

'Yes, believe it or not. Though she'll still probably take the scissors to me herself later. We clashed a few times when I was an intern. I must be a glutton for punishment, coming back to do it all again. Still, Jeremy Foster on my résumé will look pretty impressive—you can learn a lot from him.'

Alice nodded. She had been thinking absolutely the same thing when she'd applied for this rotation.

'I thought Linda was just giving me a hard time because I was pregnant,' Alice admitted.

'You're not, are you?' Josh asked feigning surprise. 'You poor old thing. My wife's expecting twins any day now— she gave up work ages ago. I have to say I admire you, taking this lot on.'

'Your wife's expecting twins?' Alice asked, unable to keep the surprise from her voice. Josh Winters looked like he should have had a surfboard under his arm, not a stethoscope around his neck. He certainly didn't fit the image of a young doctor, married with twins on the way.

'I know, I know.' He laughed, then added, 'Don't worry about old sour-grapes Linda. She's just peeved that the great Jeremy Foster is actually coming back. No one had written him off more completely than her. She was hoping for a nice fast ticket to consultant. And to make matters worse,' he said in undertones, 'Linda is the only woman in this hospital Jeremy hasn't even attempted to pull.'

'He surely can't be that bad.'

'You mark my words, he's insatiable. At least you're one female intern that doesn't have to worry about succumbing to his charms. That bump of yours will act like a crucifix to a vampire for our Jeremy, so at least you won't be putting Linda offside on that score. I hope she's shaved this morning.'

Alice found herself smiling, which was quite a revelation in itself. She hadn't been doing too much of that lately. It looked as if Josh was going to be nice to work with— heaven knew, she could use a few allies with the insatiable Jeremy and the bearded Linda breathing down her neck.

'There you are. I assume your letters of confirmation did explain it was *this* Monday you started.' Linda McFarlane's tone was anything but friendly. 'We're all waiting for you at the nurses' station.'

'You said to meet outside the ward,' Josh argued, apparently unruffled by her tones.

'I most certainly did not. What are you going to learn here? The medical students have been at the nurses' station, going through the patients notes and X-rays for half an hour now. At least *they're* showing some initiative.' And, turning on her heel, she walked smartly onto the ward.

'But she did say to meet outside,' Alice whispered furiously to Josh as they followed her onto the ward. Linda McFarlane, with her cold grey eyes and severe hairstyle, did nothing to endear herself to Alice.

'What Linda says and what she actually admits to are somewhat conflicting,' Josh said darkly. 'Watch your back.'

But Alice wasn't listening. The only back she was watching at the moment was the impeccably suited, wide-shouldered back of her new boss as he held an X-ray up to the light. His blond hair, expertly cut, tapered into his long neck. He looked as immaculately groomed and tastefully dressed as any film star from the glossies, and by hospital standards he was the closest thing to a legend Melbourne City was likely to produce.

'Finally, we can start,' Linda said pointedly, and Alice found herself holding her breath as Jeremy Foster turned and gave the briefest of smiles, his blue eyes flicking briefly down to her bulging stomach. Alice felt a small blush appear as she remembered Josh's 'vampire' comment.

'Pleased to meet you.' He held out his hand as the introductions were made, and Alice was painfully aware of her moist palms as she returned his handshake. No amount of gossip—and there had been plenty—had done him justice or even come close to adequately describing him: sun-bleached blond hair, blue eyes and an arrogant haughty smile. Momentarily stunned, she stared back at him, lost in her thoughts.

'We'll get started, then,' he said in a clipped voice, and Alice looked away, suddenly embarrassed.

She tried desperately to concentrate as they made their way around the ward, to ignore the flutter of butterflies Jeremy seemed to so effortlessly have started. Linda had the most to say—after all she had already met most of the patients and seemed to take every available opportunity to ram home how well she had coped. Jeremy didn't seem fazed by her attitude, listening intently. But every now and then he overrode a decision Linda had made or changed a drug regime, effectively assuring all present that he was the one in charge. It soon became apparent to everyone that Linda was having a lot of trouble accepting her boss's return. Her simmering resentment became increasingly obvious as they made their way around and at the final patient's bedside Linda let her bitterness surface.

'Mrs Marshall came in on Thursday with acute pancreatitis. She has a history of alcohol abuse. She's been nil by mouth on IV fluids with a pethidine infusion to control her pain. Currently, we're weaning her off the pethidine and she's now on five mls an hour. I was thinking of starting her this morning on clear fluids.'

'Good morning, Mrs Marshall. I'm Mr Foster, the surgical consultant. How are you feeling this morning?'

Mrs Marshall was struggling to sit up. 'A bit better, but I'd really like a drink of water.' Alice looked on. If this was Mrs Marshall looking better she'd have hated to have seen her on Thursday. Pancreatitis could either be acute or chronic. It caused severe abdominal pain and the patient rapidly became seriously ill. Although managed medically, it still came under the domain of the surgeons. In this case it had been precipitated by Mrs Marshall's ingestion of large quantities of alcohol.

Jeremy flicked through the patient's blood results as Mrs

Marshall fiddled in her locker. 'Her amylase levels are still very high.'

'But they've come down markedly,' Linda said.

'Still, it might be a bit early to be starting her on fluids,' Jeremy responded calmly.

'Just small sips—you can see yourself how agitated she is,' Linda pointed out. 'She's making a lot of work for the nursing staff, trying to get out of bed and get a drink.'

'Which is probably more related to her pain and her alcoholism. Keep her nil by mouth for now and increase her pethidine,' Jeremy said.

Linda pursed her lips. 'Surely we're just replacing one addiction with another. A few sips of water must be better than increasing her pethidine.'

Jeremy picked up the drug chart. 'Mrs Marshall is in pain, and that needs to be addressed. A PRN order of Valium might be wise also, given her withdrawal from alcohol.'

He turned from Linda's angry gaze and addressed the patient.

'Mrs Marshall, we're going to keep you nil by mouth for now. I know you want a drink but it really is safer not to at the moment. We'll increase your pain control and I've written up an order for some Valium which will help you to settle.'

Surprisingly, Mrs Marshall seemed a lot happier with his decision than Linda and leant back resignedly on her pillows.

'A psychiatric and social work referral would also be appropriate,' Jeremy said, handing her folder back to the charge nurse.

'She had all that last time she was in,' Linda said. 'That's why I didn't order the works this time around. She always swears she's going to give up this time, and then back she bounces.'

Jeremy nodded. 'Which, while mildly frustrating for us, must be absolute hell for Mrs Marshall and her family. See she gets the appropriate referrals.'

'Bravo, Jeremy,' Josh whispered, and Alice actually found she felt like cheering herself. Jeremy had certainly put the obnoxious Linda in her place.

'I'm not entirely happy with her.' Jeremy looked over at Alice. 'When we finish up here, can you do some blood gases on Mrs Marshall?'

'Sure.'

'I'll see you both later in pre-op clinic.' With a small nod he walked off, as Linda marched furiously behind him.

'I'll start writing up the notes, then, while you do the gases,' Josh suggested. 'Then we can grab a coffee.'

'I doubt it,' Alice said with a sigh. 'I've got three IVs to resite and a pile of drug charts that need writing up, and there's a couple of bloods that need doing.'

'Alice, Alice, Alice.' Josh gave her a wide smile. 'You have so much to learn. Fi,' he called to the charge nurse, who came over with a smile, 'this young intern hasn't yet learnt how to ask for favours. Do you think we should teach her?'

Fi smiled warmly at Alice. 'You're not listening to Josh, are you? He'll get you into all sorts of trouble.' Fi had delicate oriental features and a kind smile but, despite her seemingly easygoing nature, Alice knew just from this morning's ward round that Fi ran the ward with impeccable efficiency.

'That's not fair, Fi.' Josh winked at Alice. 'Fi and I worked together when I was a surgical intern,' he explained. 'Now, Fi, tell Alice the truth—didn't I always come at night when you paged me? Didn't I listen to you and call the reg when you were worried? Didn't I always bring doughnuts in?'

Fi nodded. 'And in return I had to do half your bloods and IVs.'

'Cheap at half the price. Come on, Fi, don't say you've gone all hard on me? You're the only reason I came back to this ward.'

Fi laughed. 'All right, I'll help with your bloods, *if* I get the time. But I'm on nights next week,' she warned, 'and you'd better remember your side of the deal.'

As Josh made his way to do his notes, Fi turned her attention to Alice, who was filling up a kidney dish with blood-gas syringes and alcohol swabs.

'When you've done the blood gases, I'll show you around,' she offered. 'Let you know how Jeremy likes things.'

'Thanks ever so much.'

Fi looked at her thoughtfully for a moment. 'Listen to me for a moment, Alice. I know I always look busy but I've always got time if you need to run something by me. If there's something you're not sure about, you can always come to me.'

Alice nodded. It was a kind offer that a lot of charge nurses made when new interns started and one that was much appreciated. Heaven knew, it was a busy enough job and you needed all the support you could get. But there was something about Fi's offer that sounded ominous, as if she almost expected trouble.

'I'd better get those gases done.'

'I'll get you some ice.'

Although Mrs Marshall was on oxygen, Alice removed the mask before she took the blood gases, as the blood taken while the patient was breathing only air would enable them to get a truer picture of her condition. Although obviously unwell, the increased pain control had already kicked in and she actually seemed in the mood for a chat.

'I'm just going to take a small sample of blood from

your wrist, Mrs Marshall, so just hold still while I inject some anaesthetic.'

'No one else has bothered with anaesthetic. How come?'

'Maybe you were too sick and they needed the blood urgently,' Alice suggested diplomatically.

'Maybe they were in too much of a hurry,' the patient said pointedly. 'When are you due?'

'In about three months' time,' Alice muttered reluctantly.

'Your first?'

Alice nodded. She really didn't want to discuss her private life with Mrs Marshall but, as she was increasingly finding out, her obvious condition seemed to be a licence for all and sundry to strike up a conversation about the most personal of subjects.

'Must be hard on your own.' She gestured to Alice's naked ring finger.

Alice concentrated on finding the pulsing artery. 'Hold still, please, Mrs Marshall.'

Thankfully she hit the jackpot first time and the bright red arterial blood spurted up the syringe.

'She got it first go and even gave me an anaesthetic first,' Mrs Marshall said loudly—to whom, Alice had no idea.

'Glad to hear it.'

Alice nearly jumped out of her skin as Jeremy made his way over. 'Let's pop your oxygen back on now.' He replaced the mask over the patient's face.

'I was just saying how hard it must be for the young doctor, being pregnant and on her own.'

Alice wished the ground would open up and swallow her, but she had no choice other than to stand there and press the cotton-wool swab for a full two minutes on the site where she had taken the arterial blood.

'Oh, I don't know,' Jeremy said lightly. 'Solitude has its virtues. I think you can stop pressing now,' he added to Alice.

Mortified, she followed him out of the room.

'Don't tell them so much next time,' Jeremy said, taking her to one side.

Alice, blushing furiously, looked down at her feet. Her tinted moisturiser had gone all blotchy. 'I'm sorry, I know it mustn't look very good—professionally, I mean—what with me being a single mother and all that.'

To her utter amazement Jeremy gave a small laugh. 'We're in the twenty-first century, Alice, for heaven's sake, not the nineteen-fifties. Nobody gives a damn these days about pregnant women being single.'

'Well, I do.' Alice said curtly, though the fact he wasn't bothered by her status was somehow strangely comforting.

'I know,' he said, and Alice looked up, surprised at his perception. 'I could tell Mrs Marshall's probing was making you uncomfortable. Next time tell them your fingers have got too fat to put your rings on, or tell them you don't want to talk about it. Tell them what you like. You're the doctor. It's you holding the consultation, not the other way around.'

'Thanks, I never thought of it like that.'

'You'd better get those blood gases over to ICU.'

Only then did Alice remember the kidney dish she was holding. 'I'll take them down to the lab myself. We're not allowed to use the ICU blood-gas machine for ward patients unless it's a real emergency,' she reminded him.

Jeremy screwed up his nose. 'Since when?'

'Since for ever—well, at least in the nine months I've been here.'

But Jeremy didn't look convinced. 'I've never had a problem. Maybe it's because I'm consultant,' he said pompously.

Well, you wouldn't have a problem, would you? Alice thought to herself as they entered the intensive care unit. One glimpse of those impossibly blue eyes and a flash of

that ready smile and everyone melted. Even Flynn, the gay-
est of porters, smoothed down his hair when Jeremy walked
past. They were all so delighted to see him that Alice stood
there awkwardly as they chatted away, greeting him like a
long-lost friend. Finally Jeremy seemed to remember why
they were there.

'I'd better get these bloods done, or we'll have to get a
fresh sample.'

Far from the grumbling staff that reluctantly allowed her
to do blood gases in only the most dire of emergencies, for
Jeremy it seemed it was absolutely no trouble at all. They
even offered to run the test for him.

'No, but thanks anyway. I just want to have a quick look
at the printout and then hopefully dash off. I'll catch you
all later.'

Alice could find neither rhyme nor reason for her indignation as she smeared a drop of blood onto the machine
and punched in her request.

'Don't take it personally,' Jeremy said, glancing at her
sideways as she glared at the machine. 'They probably let
me use the machine because they've got a bit of a soft spot
for me. I was a patient here for a while.'

Alice gave a cynical laugh as the printout appeared. The
staff might well have a soft spot for Jeremy Foster, but it
certainly wasn't all down to the fact he had been a patient
here, or even that he was a consultant.

Ripping the result off, she handed it to him.

'Better than I thought. Good. But keep an eye on her,
Alice. Given that I've upped her pethidine and prescribed
her Valium, her respiration rate could go down. Tell the
nurses to do strict one- to two-hourly obs and keep a close
eye on her oxygen saturations.'

Alice nodded.

'I'll catch you later, then.'

As he left the tiny annexe, the baby suddenly let out a

massive kick. Alice's hands instinctively moved to her stomach and she tenderly massaged it. 'Don't worry, I haven't forgotten you're in there,' she whispered, and watched out of the window as Jeremy made his way down the unit, every nurse in the place turning her head to catch a glimpse as he left. At least she didn't have to worry about Jeremy trying his well-rehearsed lines on her. Just as well really, Alice thought to herself as she made her way back to the ward. With those blue eyes and that sultry smile she doubted whether even she would be able to offer much resistance.

Pre-op clinics always ran overtime and today was no exception, given the fact it was the intern's first day and the consultant had only just returned from sick leave.

It was Alice's job to clerk the patients, which involved taking a full medical history. From there she would order any test she thought necessary prior to the patient's admission, such as ECGs and blood tests. Then the consultant would review the patient and agree or disagree with the intern's suggestions, invariably adding or removing a test. At this point, Jeremy explained, he would like her to be present.

'There's not much point otherwise. At least we can both explain our thought processes behind the pre-op work-ups. The down side is it means we won't be out of here much before six.' He gave her a sideways look. 'Or maybe even seven. Is that a problem?'

Alice shook her head. 'Sounds fine to me.'

And so they battled away. Alice took excellent histories. Somehow she managed to get the patients to open up—maybe because she gave a bit of herself back. But under her steady, unaccusing gaze the 'occasional smoker' would admit to a twenty a day habit and even the 'social drinker' admitted to a few cans mid-week. She took Jeremy's advice, though, and somehow by remembering that it was she that was holding the consultation she managed to avoid some of the more embarrassing questions that, until now, patients had assumed it was their right to ask. Not that she wasn't personable and friendly, but Marcus's rejection and her current circumstances were something Alice was having difficulty dealing with herself without the constant, however well meaning, advice from strangers.

Jeremy, on the other hand, seemed to be taking his own advice to the extreme. He was courteous, friendly even, yet he gave nothing away about himself. Every personal comment, every attempt by a patient to make small talk was immediately and skilfully rebuffed. So skilfully, in fact, that it took Alice the full afternoon to realise he never spoke about himself other than with reference to his work.

Jeremy didn't seem remotely bothered by her apparent slowness. In fact, by the time the last patient had been seen and the clock was edging towards seven, he seemed more than happy to prolong the evening with a chat.

'That's the last, Mr Foster.'

The young nurse popped her head around the door and Alice noticed her looking pointedly at her watch.

'Thanks, Emily, you did a great job today. I'm sorry we've made you so late. And, by the way, it's Jeremy.'

Instantly the bitter expression melted.

'No problem.' Emily paused. 'Jeremy. It's nice to have you back.'

That man could get away with murder, Alice thought. Why, even the most respected consultant wouldn't be left in doubt of the nurse's wrath if he let the clinic run more than two hours over, but for some reason Jeremy could get away with it. The nurses had been just as forgiving as the patients.

'I'd just like to run a couple of things by you before you go,' Jeremy said, interrupting her thoughts.

'OK.' Putting the pile of notes she had completed into the in-tray, Alice took a seat at his desk.

'You're sure?' Jeremy checked. 'You haven't got a baby-sitter you've got to get back to or anything?'

'I don't have to worry about that for a few months yet.'

'And if Mrs Marshall's observations were correct, I can assume you don't have a husband or partner wanting his dinner on the table?'

Alice swallowed nervously. She had known it would only be a matter of time before he asked. 'Another thing I don't have to worry about.'

'Good.'

Alice looked up sharply. 'Is it?'

Jeremy gave her a brief smile. 'For me it is. Look, Alice, you've heard the gossip. I'm a has-been, I'm coming back too soon, I'm half the surgeon I used to be, and all that.'

Alice flushed. 'I've heard nothing of the sort,' she lied.

'Bull.'

His expletive hit the mark. 'Well, maybe a few remarks,' she admitted. 'But you know what this place is like. Once you've been back for a couple of weeks you'll soon put them right. Anyway,' she added somewhat more forcefully, 'what on earth has any of this to do with my marital status?'

'Everything and nothing. You know how politically correct everything is these days, Alice. Apparently, I'm not supposed to notice the obvious fact that you're pregnant. And even if it's brought to my attention I'm not supposed to let it affect my judgement of you in any way. Even by having this conversation, effectively you could run off to the anti-discrimination council and have me up to my neck in hot water.'

Alice was totally confused. 'Why would I?'

'Because, as I said, your rather large bump supposedly shouldn't affect my judgement of you in the slightest.'

'And does it?' Alice asked boldly.

Jeremy stared at her for an age. Her heavy dark hair was too much for the loose scrunchy she was wearing and was slipping from its grasp, and dark grey eyes were staring up at him as if waiting for his judgement. For a second he lost his train of thought, but only for a second. His eyes flicked downwards again, and came to rest on the soft yet firm swell of her stomach.

'Yes,' he answered simply. 'Yes, it does.'

'But why? Just because I'm pregnant, it doesn't make me any less a doctor.'

Jeremy put his hands up. Tanned, manicured, long-fingered hands, Alice noticed…surgeon's hands. 'I never meant—'

But Alice interrupted him, jumping to her feet. Suddenly she felt threatened. Maybe he was about to say he didn't want her on his team, would never have agreed to it had he been in on the interview. All she knew was that it was imperative he let her stay. 'Being pregnant makes me a better doctor. I now know what it's like to lie on an examining couch and be prodded and poked. I know how it feels to be vulnerable, to be a number in the system.'

'Whoa.' Jeremy gestured for her to sit down.

Furious with herself for reacting so violently, Alice meekly did as she was told. Not trusting herself to speak, she looked up at him.

Jeremy cleared his throat before speaking. 'Firstly, I have absolutely no doubt you're a fine doctor. Your references are exemplary, and from what I've seen today you merit every word that was written. Secondly, I'm sure you really are a better doctor for being on the receiving end of the health system. I know without a shadow of doubt that I am, or at least I hope I will be. Take Mrs Marshall today. Normally I'd have dropped her pethidine down even further, and I'm not proud of that fact. But, having been in pain myself, I now recognise it all the more.' He stopped talking and for a moment Alice thought he had forgotten she was even there.

'And thirdly,' she prompted. 'I assume there's more?'

Jeremy snapped back to attention, a wry smile touching the edge of his lips. 'I'm not an obstetrician, and with good reason.'

Alice's eyebrows shot up in a questioning look.

'Heaven knows, they make enough money.'

'Tell me about it,' Alice grumbled, thinking of the invoice from Brett Halliday sitting in her bedside drawer amongst the other pile of unpaid bills.

'What I'm trying to say,' Jeremy continued, 'albeit not very well, is that pregnant women terrify me.'

Alice started to laugh, then stifled her giggle as she realised he wasn't joking.

'You're not serious?'

Jeremy nodded. 'Deadly serious. I mean, see it from my angle. If I bawl you out, are you going to burst into tears or, worse, will I induce premature labour? If I keep you behind in a clinic or call you into Theatre at midnight, am I going to do irreparable damage to the baby?'

Alice really was laughing now. 'Jeremy, I'm not a doll. I'm not some precious Ming vase that's about to shatter, for heaven's sake. I'm pregnant, that's all. Women have been managing it throughout time, in fact.'

'I know, I know. Look, I'm probably not being fair, landing this lot on you. I know you haven't asked for special favours or anything. It's just that I'm going to be pretty full-on in the ensuing months, far more so than any of the other surgeons, and that means I'm going to be asking a lot from you. I just need to know that you're up to it and if you're not I need you to tell me.'

'I'm up to it.' Alice said with conviction, but it wasn't the answer Jeremy wanted to hear.

'You still don't understand, do you?'

Alice looked at him, nonplussed. What more did he want—an affidavit?

'If I'm piling it on too thick I need to know you'll tell me. I'm single-minded where work's concerned. What I'm trying to say is that my career is everything to me. Now, I might expect loyalty and hard work from my staff and sometimes I admit I stretch the limits, but in your case you have a baby to think of. I'm not a soft touch—anything but—and I need to know that you'll tell me if there's a problem. It might not be politically correct, or whatever you want to call it, but I can't pretend your condition doesn't exist. If I'm coming down too hard, you *must* say so.'

Alice was surprised by his words, stunned even. From what she had heard of Jeremy Foster, compassion and understanding weren't on his list of credentials, and even if his attempt at these had been somewhat bumbling and massively sexist, she was touched at his attempt. 'I will,' she said softly.

'So long as we've cleared that up, then.' Jeremy gave her a dismissive nod and Alice said goodnight. Retrieving her bag from the nurses' station, it suddenly became imperative that she thank him. Making her way back to his room, she stepped inside. Jeremy was sitting there, his head in his hands. Two soluble painkillers were fizzing away in the glass next to him. From the hunch of his wide shoulders she could tell he was tense, possibly in pain. Sensing someone's presence, he sat up smartly and turned around.

'Was there anything else?'

Alice hesitated. Suddenly she felt as if she had witnessed a side that Jeremy didn't want to be seen, as if she had somehow invaded his privacy.

'I just wanted to thank you.'

'There's really no need. You'll be calling me all sorts of names by the end of the week.'

Alice gave a small smile. She knew she should go now, but for some reason she found herself standing there. He might be her consultant, but at this moment Jeremy Foster looked nothing like the dashing, confident man she had met this morning. He looked exhausted—the day must have taken its toll—and in pain, too. 'Er, is there anything I can get you?'

Jeremy gave her a quizzical look. 'Like what?'

Alice shrugged. 'A cup of tea perhaps?'

Jeremy gave a low laugh before answering sarcastically, 'A woman's solution to everything.' When Alice flushed he added more kindly, 'At least, it's my mother's solution.' He shook his head. 'I've got a headache, that's all. I'll be fine.' And, turning his back, he started dictating his notes into a machine for his secretary.

Well, what had she expected? For Jeremy Foster to confide in her, to tell her how bad he was feeling? She let out a low moan. Imagine offering him a cup of tea! Of all the stupid things to say—in one sentence she had relegated herself to the little-woman role where Jeremy so obviously thought she belonged.

If only she had known that at that same moment Jeremy's head was back in his hands and he was thinking that maybe he should have accepted that cup of tea. Maybe a few minutes spent talking to Alice would have made things a bit easier for him if he'd told her how it was for him, that the accident hadn't left him completely unscathed. That his back was killing him and he suffered headaches that were indescribable. After all, he was going to be relying a lot on her over the next few months and he was hardly about to bare his soul to Linda. And as for Josh— well, Josh was a good bloke but he gossiped far too much. Maybe talking to Alice would have helped lighten his load. But what good could have come from it? She seemed like a nice girl, but he hardly knew her. No doubt in five

minutes' flat the word would be around the hospital. Has-
been, past it, came back too soon. Jeremy pulled a face as
he downed the rest of the revolting medicine. He'd just
have to wear it for now.

CHAPTER TWO

'COULD I have a bit more light? It's like operating in a bloody dungeon here.' Alice moved the overhead light a fraction. She was too focussed on the direness of the situation to take Jeremy's comments personally.

'Dear God, why didn't they bring him in sooner?'

Alice didn't answer. She knew Jeremy was talking more to himself than to anyone else.

'More traction,' he ordered, and Alice pulled back on the retractor holding the incision Jeremy had swiftly cut further back to allow for greater visibility. She could see the sweat pouring down his forehead. No matter how many times the nurse wiped it, only seconds later he was drenched again.

He's in pain again, Alice thought, suddenly feeling sorry for him.

She had been working with Jeremy for two weeks now, and whatever Jeremy lacked in social skills he made up for in the operating room. He was quite simply the best surgeon she had ever seen. His long fingers worked deftly, his vivid blue eyes seemed to pick up the minutest detail almost before it became apparent to anyone else. But were his skills enough to save this young life?

Lachlan Scott had been wheeled into the accident and emergency department less than two hours previously. The young medical student had been complaining of abdominal pain for a couple of days now, but hadn't thought to do anything about it. Only this morning had he turned up at his father's house, vomiting and in great pain. His father, one of the leading physicians at the hospital, had immediately rushed him in. The diagnosis of appendicitis had been made even before he had hit the accident and emergency department; but it soon became clear from his rigid abdomen and shocked appearance that his appendix had already ruptured and the patient was now suffering from peritonitis. Linda and Josh had been in the middle of a hernia repair, which had left Jeremy with only the most junior of assistants.

Alice's back was killing her. Lachlan Scott had come in on the end of an already busy morning in the operating theatre, but for now her back was the least of her concerns.

'I think we're winning.' Jeremy looked up briefly and Alice could read the look of sheer relief in his vivid eyes. By the time Jeremy had stitched the last of the drains into place, which would drain any excess fluid from Lachlan's abdomen, and had covered the wound with a huge clear dressing, they had been operating for over two hours. 'Good work, everyone. Let's get him out to Recovery.'

Alice would have liked nothing more than to peel off her theatre scrubs, stand under a cool shower and follow it up with a huge mug of tea, but that luxury was going to have to wait. Lachlan had been resuscitated with fluids in the emergency department and huge doses of antibiotics had already been administered, but his post-operative IV and drug regime would have to be worked out carefully if they were to allay any of the multitude of post-operative complications he might succumb to.

'His father's just outside,' Carrie, the theatre charge nurse, prompted. Alice watched as the faintest hint of a frown appeared on Jeremy's face. 'Jeremy, he's a consultant. It will have to be you that talks to him,' Carrie said firmly.

'I know, I know,' he said irritably. 'I'll talk to him, but first I'm having a shower. I'll be back to check on Lachlan shortly.'

'Why is he so worried about talking to him?' Alice

couldn't refrain from asking when Jeremy turned on his heel and left. 'I mean, he did a brilliant job in there. You'd think he'd be the rushing off to tell Dr Scott.'

Carrie shrugged. 'Probably terrified he might have to get out his handkerchief.' She gave a small laugh and Alice heard the trace of bitterness in her voice. 'Jeremy doesn't like scenes or confrontations. If Lachlan had been a straightforward appendicitis he'd be out there now, grinning like a Cheshire cat and saying how well it had gone. You know as well as I do it's going to be pretty hard telling Lachlan's parents how sick he is. He may be out of Theatre but he certainly isn't out of the woods yet. No doubt Jeremy's hoping that by the time he's had his shower someone will have done the dirty deed for him. You'll get used to his underhand methods. I know I have.'

'I hear you've been having a bit of excitement?' Alice swung around and smiled as she saw Josh entering the recovery area. Carrie muttered something and went to check on Lachlan.

'Too much for one morning. How about you, Josh? How was your morning with Linda?'

Josh rolled his eyes. 'Bearable. At least the mask covers up her face.'

'Josh, you're terrible.' Alice giggled.

'I just say things as I see them.' He lowered his voice. 'Speaking of which, what was Carrie bitching about?'

'Nothing, she was just saying how Jeremy avoids talking to relatives when the news is bad.'

'Take everything Carrie says about Jeremy with a pinch of salt. She's just bitter because he dumped her. Or rather, he didn't dump her—he got a "friend" to do it for him.'

'Ouch,' Alice winced. 'I thought there was a bit of an undercurrent between them.'

But Josh shook his head. 'Not where Jeremy's concerned. As soon as a relationship's over, he forgets the woman ever existed and moves happily on to the next one. It's the women who are left simmering—any undercurrents come from them. Jeremy's exes probably radiate enough energy to act as the hospital's back-up generator.'

Alice's laughter was interrupted by Josh's pager. 'Now what does Linda want?' he muttered, but his face paled as he read the message.

'It's Dianne ringing,' he said, referring to his wife. Grabbing the nearest phone, he picked it up and, shaking, attempted to dial home, but kept misdialling.

'Josh, give it here.' Alice laughed. 'She probably just wants you to pick up a pizza tonight. Now, what's the number?'

But Dianne didn't want a pizza. She wanted Josh home *now* or she was going to dial for an ambulance herself.

'How far apart are the contractions?' Alice asked as Josh replaced the telephone, his face white.

'Two to three minutes apart, and from the noises she's making they're pretty full on.' He scratched his head. 'She was fine this morning, not a peep. I thought first labours went on for ever.'

'In the text books maybe, but this is real life. You'd better go now, Josh.'

'What about—?'

'*Go*,' Alice insisted. 'I'll tell Jeremy and Linda. Give me your pager. And ring me with the news,' she ordered, as he handed her his pager and notes. Josh was in such a state that he handed her his wallet. 'You don't have to pay me.' Alice laughed again.

'Wish me luck,' Josh grinned. 'Next time you see me I'll be a responsible father of two.'

Alice shook her head. 'A father, yes—responsible, no. Good luck,' she called to his rapidly departing back. And as he left Alice was suddenly filled with a hollow sadness. Josh was so excited, so ready for all that was ahead. She imagined him holding his wife's hands, working with her, guiding her through her labour. And afterwards, when their babies were born, sharing in each other's joy, united as a family. Her hand moved down to the solid swell beneath her theatre greens. Her baby was missing out on so much. And that hurt Alice, not for herself but for her unborn baby.

Maybe lots of women had babies without a partner these days, some even by choice, but it had never been her intention. She had always assumed that when—if—the time came to have children, it would be with the man she loved at her side. She knew the pain she felt now would only magnify with time. It had been hard enough at the antenatal classes, listening as the midwife had explained the role of the partner during labour. Alice had felt the weight of the pitying smiles then as she had sat alone, pretending to take notes.

What would it be like when she was actually *in* labour? When the pain got too much and there was no one she knew there to comfort her, to guide her and cheer her on? And then… Alice closed her eyes as they started to fill. How would it feel when the baby was born and there was no one to share it with, no one to gloat with and gaze in wonder at the miracle of birth?

'He's waking up.'

Alice snapped back to attention at Carrie's words, and made her way over to the gurney.

'What are his obs doing?'

'Stable. His blood pressure's good, still febrile and his temp's thirty-eight.'

'We'll just have to wait for the antibiotics to kick in. Lachlan, it's Dr Masters. I saw you briefly in the accident department. Lie still now, Lachlan, you're just coming to after an operation.' Alice kept her voice low and steady, trying to orientate and at the same time reassure the young man.

The anaesthetist had entered and was setting up a peth-idine infusion for Lachlan. For the immediate post-op pe-riod a high dose of analgesic would be administered auto-matically, to control his pain, but as his consciousness and condition improved he would be using a patient controlled analgesia machine which would enable him to administer a safe dose of analgesic to himself as required.

'How's he doing?' Jeremy asked. Looking refreshed from his shower and, as usual, immaculately presented, he accepted the chart from Carrie. His question was directed more at the anaesthetist than Alice.

'Happy from this end. Where are you sending him?'

'There's a HDU bed on Surgical 1.'

'Josh's wife rang,' Alice informed him. 'Apparently—'

'I know already,' Jeremy answered, without looking up. 'I collided with him on my way here.'

And that was that. No small talk, no casual remarks about wishing him well, or the usual groan about twins. Jeremy obviously wasn't remotely interested.

'He said he's left his pager with you.' The blue eyes turned to her and Alice nodded.

'Well, if it gets too much, let Linda know. She'll have to pitch in.'

Which was about as helpful as suggesting she ring Josh if there were any problems. There was as much chance of Linda resiting an IV as Josh leaving his wife's side.

'How were Lachlan's family?' Carrie asked.

'Upset, relieved—the usual. I said they could pop in for two minutes before we transfer him.'

But Carrie wasn't having any of it. 'You know the rules. They'll have to wait until he's transferred to the ward, like every other family has to. Just because his father's a con-sultant here—'

'His father's not the only consultant here,' Jeremy re-minded her. 'If you're so against staff having the occasional perk, like seeing their critically ill son in the recovery room, maybe it's just as well you work in the operating room, Carrie. Your personality wouldn't go down too well with a conscious patient.'

Alice watched as Carrie's shoulders stiffened, two spots of colour burning on her angry, taut cheeks. And though Alice knew Carrie had been out of line, the way she had addressed Jeremy, she actually felt sorry for her. Jeremy might have been a consultant, but he had by all accounts been more to her than that, and from her reaction towards him it wasn't all over where Carrie was concerned.

'Any news on Josh?'

Alice shook her head as she made her way over to Fi, who was coming out from handover. 'Not yet. I suppose he's got a million relatives and friends to ring before he gets around to letting us know.'

Fi shrugged. 'Dianne's probably still in labour. Looks like it's going to be a long hard night for womankind to-night. I suppose you're covering for Josh as well as your own work?'

'Linda's going to help out,' Alice said without much enthusiasm.

'Like I said, it's going to be a long hard night.'

Alice wasn't given to moaning about her colleagues, but Fi's inference was so spot on that Alice couldn't help but give a small smile. 'I bought some doughnuts,' she said holding out a brown paper bag, which Fi accepted with a laugh.

'Then what have I got to moan about? I'd better start doing the drugs. How about you? Do you need anything?'

Alice shook her head. 'I'm pretty much up to date. I've got a couple of bloods to do at eleven so I'll be back then. I'm going to head down to A and E—there's a couple of patients Linda wants to admit that need to be clerked before they can be sent up to the ward, and then…' Her voice trailed off as Jeremy and Linda walked through the ward doors.

'Bit late for a ward round,' Fi muttered.

'How's Lachlan Scott doing?' Jeremy enquired.

'His temperature's come down and his obs are stable,' Alice answered. 'I just left him.'

'Good. We're just going to have a quick look before I head off.'

'Sure.'

But though Linda headed off to the HDU section, Jeremy just stood there. 'Er, I was wondering if I could have a word?'

'I'll get on with the drugs,' Fi said cheerfully, but Jeremy shook his head. 'With both of you, please. Fi, do you mind if we go into your office?' Not waiting for an answer, he led the way. Fi and Alice followed, a worried look passing between the two women. There must be a problem on the ward they didn't know about. 'Sit down, please.'

Alice felt as if she were being hauled into the headmaster's office for a telling-off, but when she finally looked up at Jeremy she realised that he wasn't angry.

'I'm afraid I've got some bad news.'

Alice swallowed nervously.

'What?' Fi asked bluntly.

'It would seem that Dianne's labour wasn't very straightforward.'

Alice felt a cold shiver run down her spine.

'Apparently, the first twin, a little boy, was delivered successfully, but there were problems getting the second twin out.'

'Shoulder dystocia?' Fi asked, her voice shaky, referring to a condition in labour where a baby's shoulders have difficulty negotiating the bony pelvis.

Jeremy shook his head. 'No, Josh wasn't very clear on

the telephone but it would seem the second twin just didn't descend at all. They had to use forceps, but they couldn't get a grip. They made a number of attempts…'

Alice winced at the thought, and Jeremy shot her a look.

'Sorry, you probably don't need to hear all the details.'

But Alice shook her head fiercely 'No, tell me. I'm all right.'

'Well,' he continued tentatively, 'it would seem by the time they delivered the second twin, another little boy, he wasn't breathing and there was no output. He had to be resuscitated. Apparently it was rather lengthy, though they did get him back. Anyway, the upshot is that the baby's pretty sick. He's on PICU. He's bruised and battered from the forceps and he's got some breathing difficulties.'

'Poor Josh,' Alice whispered, almost to herself. 'And poor Dianne,' she added. Although she had never met Dianne, her heart went out to this woman and the pain she must be feeling.

'Obviously Josh will be taking some time off, which is going to mean more work for you, Alice.'

'I'll be fine,' she said, her grey eyes brimming with tears. 'It kind of puts things into perspective, doesn't it?'

Jeremy gave a brief nod. He wasn't going to be drawn into a deep discussion, but she could tell from his eyes that this news had shaken him, too.

It was a rather subdued group that made their way quietly out of the office. Linda was breaking the news rather less tactfully to the anaesthetic registrar.

'Which is just great. We've got the consultant just back from sick leave, the reg on annual leave, the resident on paternity leave and the intern about to go on maternity leave. I'm carrying the lot of them.'

'That's what I like about you, Linda,' Jeremy said dryly, as the anaesthetic reg signalled a desperate look at Linda to stop. 'Your sense of team spirit.' And without a backward glance he made his way across to Lachlan Scott, leaving Linda spluttering her excuses to his departing back.

Blinking back tears, Alice made her way down to A and E. How could it all have gone so terribly wrong? She remembered Josh's excited face just this morning. Oh, she knew things went wrong, that there were no guarantees of a perfect healthy baby, but why did it have to happen? And why to Josh and Dianne? It just wasn't fair.

A and E was busy, but wasn't it always?

'Hi, Alice.' Fay, the Unit Manager greeted her.

'Hi, Fay. I didn't expect to see you. How come you're on nights?'

'Don't ask.' Fay rolled her eyes. 'Given the fact that it's me who does the roster, I guess I've only got myself to blame. Anyway, it might be chaotic down here, but from a surgical point of view it's not too bad. There's just two for you to clerk in. Linda's seen them and ordered a few tests, but most can wait for the morning. As soon as you're done I can shift them up to the ward and free up a couple of trolleys.'

Which was an extremely nice way of saying 'get on with it'.

So she did, or at least she tried to, but no sooner had she clerked the first patient and was about to start with the second one than the sound of her pager signalled the end of her introduction to the patient.

'I'm sorry, Mr West, I'll just have to answer this. I'll be back to clerk you, hopefully soon.'

'No worries, love.'

Dialing the number as she flicked through Mr West's medical history, she was surprised when Fi answered. Normally Fi held off from paging when she knew Alice was coming back. Something must be up.

'I haven't forgotten the bloods, Fi. I've just got one more patient to clerk then I'll be up.'

But that wasn't why Fi was ringing. 'I've already done your bloods, so don't worry about that. Look, Alice, I'm a bit worried about Lachlan Scott. Would you mind coming and having a look?'

Alice didn't need to be asked twice. Ignoring the pained look from Fay, she made her way straight up to the ward.

'Thanks,' Fi said when Alice arrived. 'Hopefully I'm worrying about nothing, but he just doesn't seem right to me.'

'What are his obs doing?' Alice asked as they made the way to his bedside.

'Nothing remarkable. His temp's normal and his blood pressure's a tiny bit low, but I guess that could be put down to his analgesia.'

Lachlan Scott looked pretty much the same as when Alice had last seen him, maybe a little paler but nothing that would cause Alice too much concern. 'Lachlan, I'm just going to have a look at you,' Alice informed him, as Fi and Kate, the student nurse, helped her with the bedclothes. Lachlan gave a small nod.

'How are you feeling, Lachlan?' Alice asked.

'Tired.'

'Are you in any pain?'

Not bothering to open his eyes, Lachlan shook his head as Alice gently palpated his abdomen. Again there was no real change since the last time she'd seen him. Listening to his chest, she found the story was the same—nothing remarkable.

But Fi was worried and Alice wasn't going to ignore the fact.

Suddenly Lachlan opened his eyes. 'I should be in the library. I've got an exam in the morning.'

Alice gave Fi a worried glance.

'Lachlan, do you know where you are?' Fi asked urgently.

Closing his eyes, Lachlan nodded.

'Where, Lachlan?'

'Melbourne City.' Which, of course, was the right an-swer, but his moment of confusion prompted Alice into action.

'Do another set of obs and I'll ring Linda.'

Linda was particularly unhelpful. 'So let me get this straight. His obs are fine, and you can't find anything wrong on examination. Exactly why are you calling me, Alice?'

'Because the nursing staff are concerned—I'm con-cerned,' she said trying to sound confident. 'And, as I said, he's confused.'

'Momentarily,' Linda pointed out. 'He's had major sur-gery, he's on a high dose of pethidine and you've just woken him up in the middle of the night. You said yourself he's orientated now. Look, Alice, I just had A and E on the telephone complaining there's still a patient waiting to be clerked. I'm stuck on Intensive Care with a sick patient and I've still got a list of patients to see on the wards. Now you're ringing to tell me a patient I reviewed an hour ago is in the exact same condition as when I left.'

'I'd just like you to review him,' Alice said as evenly as she could. 'I'd really value your opinion,' she added tact-fully.

'When I get a moment,' was all Linda could offer.

'Is she coming?' Fi asked as Alice replaced the receiver.

'When she gets time.' Alice shrugged. 'What are his obs doing now?'

'Not much change. His temp's down a bit further—it's 35.0 now.' Which was low. Not dangerously low, but low enough to set an alarm bell ringing in Alice's head.

'He could be septic.'

'But wouldn't his temperature be high then?' Kate asked.

Alice shook her head. 'Not necessarily. Sometimes when

the body's overwhelmed with infection a patient can actually become *hypo*thermic.'

Alice wasn't a brilliant doctor, she was the first to admit that. She had got into and through medical school by sheer hard work and diligence. But she was a good doctor, and she knew that, too. And part of being a good doctor involved listening. Fi, with her years of knowledge and experience, had called on her because she was worried, and now Alice was worried as well. She wrung her hands anxiously. 'I'd better ring Jeremy.' She looked at Fi for her reaction.

'Good. I'll share the flak if it's nothing.'

She had obviously woken him when she'd rung, and Jeremy listened without interruption as she relayed her findings.

'What did Linda say?'

'She's a bit busy at the moment. His temperature wasn't quite so low, though, when I spoke to her,' Alice said hesitantly. 'Maybe I should have called her back…'

'Doesn't matter now. Look, take some gases and bloods, do some cultures as well, and I'll be straight in.'

Alice, unsure whether her concern for the patient was entirely merited, was somewhat taken aback by how amenable he was being. 'I could ring Linda again,' she offered. 'Or call you back with the blood results. It could be nothing.'

'Let's hope it is,' Jeremy said darkly. 'I'm on my way.'

Linda wasn't all bad, and in fairness she did come over almost immediately. But Alice's relief at seeing her senior quickly vanished when Linda heard she had already contacted Jeremy.

'You *what*? You just went ahead and called him? How dare you, without running it by me first?'

Alice was trying to concentrate on finding a vein and didn't look up as she answered. 'I did run it by you first. I felt Lachlan needed to be seen, and urgently. I knew how busy you were.'

'So you went straight over my head?'

Alice didn't reply; she was becoming increasingly worried about Lachlan now. His veins were proving extremely difficult to find, again a rather ominous sign in a young healthy man.

'It's not your responsibility to ring the consultant. You ring me and then *I* decide. It's not your concern…'

Alice had heard enough. Rowing at a sick patient's bedside really wasn't her style. 'I'm paid to be concerned, Linda, and right now I'd appreciate your help in finding a vein. You can bawl me out later.'

'Let's concentrate on the patient, shall we?' Jeremy's rich tones filled the room, and Linda immediately snapped to attention.

'You got here quickly,' Fi said appreciatively.

'I'm sleeping at the hospital tonight.'

Alice's eyebrows shot up in surprise but she didn't say anything.

In the short space of time it had taken Jeremy and Linda to arrive, it had become obvious that Lachlan was extremely unwell. He kept pulling off his oxygen mask, confused rantings coming from his mouth.

'Linda, run over to ICU and get the gases done,' Jeremy said quickly. 'Fi, call a MET.'

Fi nodded and turned to Kate. 'You do it. Tell them the room number and bring back the resusc trolley with you.'

As the overhead chimes relayed their urgent message, Alice felt her adrenaline kick into overdrive. A medical emergency team was called when a patient was suffering a life-threatening incident. It was a relatively new innovation, and not practised at many hospitals, but it had on many occasions proved to be more than effective. Once the call was put out, the ICU anaesthetist, along with an ICU nurse and the on-call physicians, would make their way urgently to the patient's bedside to implement urgent intervention *before* the patient arrested. And though it was becoming increasingly obvious to Alice that Lachlan really was very sick, she was somewhat surprised at the dramatic measure Jeremy had taken.

From then on Alice felt she was somewhat supernumerary as a multitude of staff and equipment appeared, all far more skilled and experienced at coping with emergencies than she was. Jeremy relayed the findings to the MET team as IV fluids were pumped into Lachlan's system and his oxygen concentration was turned up. The head of the bed had been removed by Fi to allow the anaesthetist more access to Lachlan's airway, and the patient was now attached to a cardiac monitor with a probe clipped onto his earlobe to continually measure his oxygen saturation.

'Ring the lab, Alice, and ask them to step on his bloods,' Jeremy ordered, just as Linda returned breathlessly with his blood gas results.

'We'll get him over to ICU,' the anaesthetist addressed Jeremy. 'We'll need to put in a central line and do the works, but hopefully the antibiotics will kick in soon. It's lucky we got to him in time. That was a good pick-up, Jeremy. Glad to have you back on board.'

By the time Lachlan had been wheeled over to ICU it was a white, shaking Alice that stood in the empty room as Fi started to clear up the large mess that had been created. ICU wasn't Alice's domain. It was up to her to cover the rest of the wards.

'That was close,' Fi said.

'Very,' agreed Alice. 'He just seemed to go downhill so quickly.'

Fi nodded. 'Young, fit ones often do that. They hold their vital signs stable until the last minute. By the time a young guy like that drops his BP you're often too late. I'm sure there's a far more technical way of explaining it, but I'll leave that for Jeremy to explain.'

'Thanks, Fi, if it hadn't been for you…'

'Don't sell yourself short. It took a lot of guts to ring Jeremy.'

They both looked up simultaneously as Jeremy coughed, making his presence known.

'I agree.'

Alice didn't answer.

'How's Lachlan?' Fi asked. 'Will he be going back to Theatre?'

Jeremy shook his head. 'Not at this stage. He's had an ultrasound and it doesn't look as if there's a collection in his abdomen. He's septic from the infection, we think. Hopefully we can keep him going until the antibiotics kick in. His parents have arrived. I was wondering if you could come in with me, Fi?'

Fi nodded. 'I'll take them down to the day room.'

'You might as well head off to bed, Alice,' Jeremy said, without meeting her eyes.

'I've still got a patient in A and E to clerk.'

'Don't worry about that,' Jeremy said, rather too lightly. 'I've rung A and E and they're going to send him straight up—he can be clerked later. Linda's going to be up all night with me, anyway. I can tell her to head over here and do it when there's time. Is there anything else outstanding?'

'Just some two a.m. bloods.' She glanced at her watch. 'Which are just about due.'

'I'm sure Fi can help with that. If not, I'll come and do them.'

'You?' Alice said rather ungraciously. Since when did a consultant offer to do an intern's two a.m. bloods? 'Are you sure?'

'I'm sure I can handle it,' Jeremy said in his superior way, and then his tones softened. 'Let's say I owe you one.

Linda, too, for that matter,' he added darkly. A ghost of a smile touched his lips. 'Go on, get some rest. You might even cram in a couple of hours' sleep.'

It was then that Alice noticed how pale Jeremy looked. The night's events had obviously shaken him up as well.

'Thanks, then,' she said gratefully. 'But call if you need me.'

As she made her way out of the room Jeremy called her back.

'Likewise, Alice. You call if you need me as well. I'll always listen.'

Never had the thin, hard, on-call bed looked more tempting. Aching and exhausted, Alice slipped off her shoes and slowly lowered herself onto the mattress. Normally she slept on her stomach, but her ever-increasing size had meant that for the last few weeks she had been forced to sleep on her back or side, which inevitably meant most of the night was spent tossing and turning, trying to get comfortable. With a groan she placed her pager on the bedside table and flicked off the lamp, tucking a plastic-covered hospital pillow under her bump she rolled onto her side. A couple of hours sounded good from here. There was still a full day's work tomorrow to get through. Fancy Jeremy telling her to go to bed. Under normal circumstances she would have insisted she was fine, but Brett Halliday's warnings had hit home and she wasn't going to do anything to risk her health—too much depended on it. Anyway, given how the night's events had panned out, Linda probably *did* owe her one, Alice mused. Still, it had been extremely nice of Jeremy to pull rank and, in his own way, to thank her. But, then, that was how Jeremy had been all the time she had worked for him—extremely nice. Low as her expectations had been about his demeanour, he had surprised her. Drifting off into a deep sleep, her last conscious thoughts were of Jeremy, and as her subconscious kicked in, her dreams for once were not filled with Marcus and unborn babies, but a certain consultant with blond hair and a smile that set her heart racing.

CHAPTER THREE

'Good morning, Dr Masters, your six a.m. alarm call.'

'But I didn't book one,' Alice replied, fuddled and confused. Flicking on the light, she reached for her watch, trying to orientate herself to her surroundings. With a jolt of panic she reached for her pager. 'Has anyone been trying to get hold of me?'

'Not as far as I know,' the switchboard operator answered cheerfully. Replacing the receiver, Alice sat up slowly.

'Good morning to you, too,' she said, as the baby let out a huge kick.

Standing under the shower jets, Alice closed her eyes as the warm water slowly brought her around. Four solid hours' sleep on an on-call night was a luxury she hadn't even dared dream about. Thank goodness the switchboard operator had called, Alice thought. She was so tired she might have slept in until midday. Pulling on some fresh greens, she made her way down to the canteen, but the bleeping of her pager foiled any thought of lingering over a cooked breakfast. After purchasing a muesli bar and a coffee from the machine, she made her way over to the surgical unit.

'Morning, Fi, how has it been?'

Fi rolled her eyes. 'Let's just say I'm glad it's morning. Nothing for you to worry about, though,' Fi said quickly as Alice gave a concerned look. 'Just a couple of the old dears decided to go a-wandering. It must be a full moon. Anyway...' She grinned. 'You certainly look a lot better. Did you have a good sleep?'

'Marvellous. Luckily, switchboard gave me a wake-up call or I'd still be there now. You didn't book it by any chance?' Alice asked, but Fi shook her head.

'Maybe Linda was having an attack of the guilts. She looked positively sheepish when she came over to do some bloods. I was going to page you to resite an IV and Linda even said that she'd do it—I nearly fainted with surprise. Who knows? Lachlan Scott going off like that might be just the jolt Linda needed to bring her back down to earth.'

'Maybe,' Alice said, but she was far from convinced. Linda McFarlane might have had a bit of a jolt, but Alice was quite sure it would take more than that to soften the edges. Though not a vindictive person, Alice had a sharp memory, and Linda would need to do more than take a few bloods and book a wake-up call to earn Alice's respect. 'How's Lachlan doing—have you heard?'

'Stable. Jeremy's been in with him all night. Apparently his cultures already show a massive infection. It's lucky we got him over to ICU when we did. I wouldn't have fancied his chances otherwise.'

'Unbelievable.' Alice let out a small sigh. 'People are so sure an appendectomy is just a minor operation these days, which, of course, it would have been if Lachlan had come in earlier.'

Fi nodded and added in a subdued voice, 'Like having twins. With IVF and everything, twins are so much more common but people just don't realise the dangers of multiple births. I remember when I did my midwifery, everyone was on standby when twins were about to be delivered. It seems almost a non-event these days—until it all goes wrong, that is.'

'Have you heard anything?'

'I rang just before. Obviously they wouldn't tell me much, but apparently there's not much change. We'll just have to wait for more detail. I'm sure Josh will let us know more when he can.'

But Josh didn't ring. And by five o'clock, when the euphoria of four hours' sleep had long since worn off and Alice sat exhausted as the tram clattered along, the sight of the Women's and Children's was something she just couldn't go past. Despite the fact she had only known Josh two weeks, and had never met his wife, Josh had shown her so much kindness. She wouldn't be nosy, wouldn't ask to see the babies or anything like that. She simply wanted to let them know they were in her thoughts. If the roles had been reversed—and, please, God, they wouldn't be, Alice thought, instinctively placing a protective hand over her stomach—she just *knew* Josh would do the same. Jeremy, despite his obvious sadness as he'd broken the news, hadn't mentioned Josh all day. Babies were obviously way down on his list of priorities.

And as for Linda… Alice's lips thinned just at the thought of her. Linda might well have been more pleasant today, but the daggers coming from her icy eyes hadn't gone unnoticed by Alice. Her first impressions about Linda, Alice concluded, had been right, and she wasn't about to be fooled. One thing she prided herself on was being an excellent judge of character—except with Marcus, she reminded herself ruefully.

Not just Marcus, Alice thought in surprise as the lift doors opened to the maternity section. She had been rehearsing what to say. Her plan had been to ask at the nurses' station if she could have a word with Josh in the corridor. Jeremy had obviously had the same idea.

Both men turned as she made her way along the carpeted floor towards them.

'I hope you're here to see me and not looking for the delivery room?' Josh smiled. But despite the welcoming, half-joking words and the apparently casual hug, Alice knew he was devastated. His eyes were swollen and red-rimmed and he held onto her tightly for a second before letting her go.

'Hopefully not for a few weeks yet, Josh. How are you and Dianne doing?' She was terrified to ask after the twins in case the news had become worse.

'Holding up. Dianne's been marvellous. She's exhausted, though. Insisting on expressing milk and sitting in the intensive care unit. The nurses have just given her a couple of sleeping tablets so hopefully she'll get a few hours' rest.'

'How are the boys?' Alice asked finally.

'Declan's great,' he swallowed hard. 'I was just telling Jeremy it's not so good for Eamon.' Alice looked up at Jeremy for the first time and gave a small nod of greeting. Turning back to Josh, she was horrified to see huge tears splashing down his cheeks. 'It doesn't look too great,' Josh said, his words strangled as he tried to control his emotions.

Alice put a comforting hand on his arm. 'It's all right Josh. You don't have to go through it all for me. Jeremy can tell me. I just came to see how *you* were doing. To see if there was anything I could do to help.'

She felt so helpless standing there.

'Actually, there is something,' Josh said.

'Tell me,' Alice urged.

A hint of a blush crept over Josh's freckled face. 'Well, we left in rather a rush, as you know. Dianne didn't bring her...' He paused. 'You know... There's a chemist down in the foyer. Would you mind, Alice?'

'For heaven's sake, Josh!' It was the first time Jeremy had spoken. 'I thought you were a new age kind of guy.'

'I know, I know.' Josh replied, blushing ever deeper. 'How would you like having to buy them? That would ruin your cool image a bit, wouldn't it?'

The light-hearted jostling was a welcome relief after the previous tension.

'There's nothing to it,' Jeremy insisted. 'I'll be back in five. Get him a sandwich or something, will you, Alice? I've tried and he won't eat a thing. Maybe a woman will have more luck. He looks as if he's about to faint.'

Once Jeremy had gone Alice linked an arm through one of Josh's. 'You heard the boss. Come on, you need to eat.'

At the entrance the women's auxiliary had a small stall, selling drinks and snacks along with an assortment of hand-knitted baby goods and handmade teddy bears. Balloons with congratulatory messages for a baby boy, girl...twins adorned the stall.

Josh eyed them ruefully as Alice returned with a sandwich for Josh and two coffees.

'Not a ''get well soon'' balloon in sight,' Josh said pensively. 'You just never think it's going to go so wrong.'

Alice recalled Fi's words of that morning but didn't say anything, allowing Josh to continue.

'That's not strictly true. I imagined every possible scenario but deep down I just thought I was worrying unnecessarily, that everything would be fine.'

Alice put a hand over Josh's cold one. 'That's what we all do, Josh. You'd go crazy otherwise. But you also know deep down that, whatever happens, you'll deal with it. It's not as if we have much choice in these things.'

Josh stared into his coffee for a few minutes. 'Fancy Jeremy coming up to see me. He told me not to worry about work, to take all the time I needed. He's a good egg, Jeremy, despite what everyone says.'

'You really like him, don't you?' Alice asked, unable to keep the hint of surprise out of her voice. She was so used to hearing Jeremy derided.

'I think he's great; I always have. Why do you sound so surprised?'

Alice shrugged, not sure what to say. 'He's got such a

reputation. I mean, I know he's a great surgeon, but he's stepped on a lot of toes.'

Josh grinned. 'In his rush to get to the bedroom. Look, beneath all that smooth talk is a nice guy. Hell, if I looked like that…'

'Here you go.' Jeremy thrust a huge carrier bag into Josh's lap. 'Told you—nothing to it.'

'Jeremy.' Josh laughed. 'You've practically bought out the whole shop. 'Toothpaste, teddies, deodorant—did you hide the sanitary pads under them in the basket?'

This time it was Jeremy who blushed. 'I got them, didn't I?'

'Dr Winters.' Josh jumped as a midwife came over. 'Calm down, there's no change,' the midwife said quickly, seeing the look of utter panic on Josh's face. 'But Declan is awake and screaming at the top of his voice. Dianne will be out for a few hours yet. I thought you might like to give Declan some of Dianne's milk.'

Josh nodded eagerly. 'I'll be right there.' He gave a grateful smile. 'Thanks for coming by guys, it meant a hell of a lot.' He gave Alice a quick hug and shook Jeremy's hand before rushing off to the nursery.

Alice sat shyly after he had left.

'Hungry?' Jeremy asked.

'A bit. I might grab a sandwich myself. I can't be bothered to cook.'

'Hardly good for the baby, is it?'

Alice gave him a surprised look. 'You're an expert on maternal nutrition, are you? Actually, I was going to grab a beef and spinach foccacia. Full of iron.'

Jeremy screwed up his nose. 'Not by the time the women's auxiliary get hold of it. Come on, we'll go and grab something a bit more nutritious *and* tasty.'

His invitation was so casual it could hardly even be

called that, and Alice knew she would look stupid if she turned him down, and yet…

'Come on,' he said irritably, as she hesitated. 'Where are you parked?'

'I haven't got a car,' Alice answered. 'I came on the tram.'

'Good, that makes it easier,' Jeremy replied.

Oh, well, she thought as she picked up her bag, what choice did she have?

Sitting beside Jeremy in his slick car made Alice feel positively claustrophobic. The seats were impossibly low and Jeremy had to help her with the seat belt, which Alice rightly assumed hadn't been designed with a pregnant woman in mind. Never had she felt so huge and unattractive, and never had she been more acutely aware of the fact that Jeremy Foster was every inch a man—his expensive suit brushing her arm, the weight of him as he leant across her, the subtle scent of his cologne mingling with the heavy scent of his maleness. Alice flattened herself against the seat in a vain attempt to appear thinner, and after a couple of attempts Jeremy managed to create enough slack in the seat belt to get the beastly strap across her huge stomach. Alice thought she would die of embarrassment.

She was also painfully aware that all she had in her purse was a fifty-dollar note which she had hoped to use as a deposit for a crib. The way Jeremy had sneered at the sandwiches the women's auxiliary had on offer didn't allow Alice to hold out much hope that they would be stopping at the nearest burger bar. She was right. Sliding the car into a space directly in front of the Hyatt Hotel, Jeremy jumped out as the doorman opened the car door for Alice. Hardly stopping to retrieve his receipt, Jeremy casually strolled up the entrance steps.

'How come he's parking it for you?' Alice asked, bewildered. 'Are you a guest here?'

'Might as well be, the amount of times I eat here.'

At least the Hyatt had a massive food court. Perhaps she could steer him towards the noodles. Jeremy, of course, baulked at the idea.

'I've either been standing in Theatre or Intensive Care all day. If you think I'm going to stand in line for my dinner, you're mistaken. Come on.'

Alice bristled. He was so haughty, so arrogant and superior. How dared he just assume she wanted to sit in some five-star restaurant and dine with him?

Her acrimony didn't last long. Lowering herself into a sumptuous seat, she caught his eye and Jeremy gave her the benefit of his perfect white smile. Murder—again that was the thought that sprang to mind; this man could get away with murder. But she did have her credit card on her. OK, she had sworn it was for emergencies only, but what was this? It was hardly everyday stuff, sitting in a luxury restaurant with the most gorgeous of men, who also happened to be your boss.

Oh, well, when in Rome and all that. If she was going to use her credit card it might as well be for the benefit of the baby, Alice thought as she ordered a well-done steak with fresh garden vegetables.

Jeremy chose red snapper.

'Would sir like to see the wine list?'

Without looking up, Jeremy shook his head. 'I'll just have a mineral water, thanks. Alice?'

'The same for me, please.'

By the time their drinks had appeared, bread had been served and the wineglasses removed, Alice felt her butterflies start to disappear.

'How are you finding it?' Jeremy asked.

Alice smiled. 'Lovely. You were right. I'm sick of hospital sandwiches.'

'I meant work.'

Alice flushed. 'Oh.' The waiter appeared again and swapped Alice's knife for a steak knife. 'Work's fine, too,' she said once they were alone again.

'But not lovely?'

'I could think of other words to describe last night.'

Jeremy looked at her thoughtfully. 'I've spoken to Linda. She was always going to come, you know.'

'No, Jeremy, I didn't know,' Alice said forcefully, for the first time staring directly at him. 'I'm not interested in mind games. I accept that I'm a very junior doctor; I've got no delusions of grandeur on that count. When I rang Linda for help and she gave no indication that she was coming in time, I had to make a choice. At the end of the day it wouldn't have stood up too well in the Coroner's Court if I stated that I assumed she'd be coming and did nothing.'

Jeremy winced. 'Thank God it didn't come to that. He's a lot better this evening.'

Alice took a sip of her drink. 'Good. Look, Jeremy, to her credit, Linda did come—'

Jeremy interrupted her. 'But next time you'll think twice about ringing her?''

'Exactly. Which isn't the safest of situations.'

Jeremy stared at her thoughtfully. 'Which is why, and this is strictly between you and me, I ripped a strip off Linda last night. She *is* a good doctor, but she's got a lot to learn—mainly about how to treat her colleagues. Now, I think last night shook her up, so hopefully she'll lift her game. But don't worry, I'll be watching things closely. And if ever you are worried, I need you to promise me that you *will* ring Linda without hesitation, and if you get no joy ring me straight away. Don't jeopardise your career for the sake of ruffling a few feathers.'

'You don't have to worry about that,' Alice said seriously. 'I have no intention of jeopardising either my career or the patients' well-being. You've got no concerns there.'

'I know.'

Glad they'd at least got that out of the way, Alice started to eat the meal which had just arrived, but any thoughts of polite small talk flew out of the window when Jeremy voiced his next question. 'So, how did you get pregnant?'

Alice nearly choked on her steak. 'I beg your pardon?' she finally managed to get out when she had finished coughing. 'I would have thought that you of all people would know by now where babies come from.'

Jeremy grinned but pressed on, unfazed. 'It's a natural question to ask. Was it planned?'

'That's none of your business,' Alice retorted furiously, her eyes watering. 'You were the one who said I didn't have to reveal anything I didn't want to.'

'But that was to the patients,' Jeremy answered straightforwardly. 'I'm a friend.'

Alice looked at him, bemused. 'You're a colleague. You're my boss.'

'All right, then.' Jeremy shrugged. 'We can talk about me instead. I'm good at that.'

Again he flashed his impossible smile and Alice managed a small one back. Oh, well, what was the harm in telling him? It was hardly a state secret.

'It wasn't planned,' she admitted. 'I'd have thought that was obvious.'

'Some women choose to go it alone.' He leant over the table but didn't bother to lower his voice. 'My mother knows someone who's a ''miss'' in every sense of the word. Apparently she's found some guy who's prepared to donate—'

Alice put up her hand. 'Spare me the details.' She flushed as a smirking waiter refilled her water glass.

Jeremy laughed, and there was something about the refreshing directness of his question that made Alice tentatively start to open up. In between mouthfuls of the most delicious steak she had tasted in years, she found herself filling Jeremy in on the most painful intimate details of her life.

'Marcus and I were going out for two years. We'd never really spoken about marriage, but I just assumed it would happen one day. He was a dental student and we were both at the same uni in Adelaide. Marcus had big plans. He was going to take over his uncle's dental practice here in Melbourne—'

'And what about you?' Jeremy cut in.

'I'd do my internship here and then specialise.'

'In what?' Jeremy asked.

'I liked paeds,' Alice admitted. 'That was my first rotation, although A and E holds a certain fascination. It was paeds that got me into this mess.'

Jeremy raised his eyebrows but didn't interrupt again.

'We had a little girl in who was extremely unwell,' Alice explained. 'It turned out she had meningococcal meningitis. A few of us had been pretty hands-on with her so it was recommended that we take some antibiotics.'

'You surely knew that they interfere with the Pill, or at the very least the pharmacist should have warned you.'

'Yes to both,' Alice gave a resigned smile. 'The problem was that Marcus wasn't due to be in Melbourne for a fortnight so I assumed that the warnings didn't apply to me and promptly forgot them. When Marcus turned up for the weekend for a ''surprise'' visit it never even entered my head I might get pregnant.'

'What did Marcus say?'

Alice fiddled with the food on her plate before answering. 'A lot. But the long and the short of it was that he wanted me to have an abortion, and that's a polite way of putting it.'

'But you didn't—obviously?'

Alice shrugged. 'I'd love to say it never entered my head, but I'd be lying. I even made an appointment, but at the end of the day I just couldn't do it. Marcus was furious, said that I'd ruined all his plans for us, that children weren't on his agenda for years yet. I think he had a vision of us as a couple of yuppies, bringing in the big bucks and living in a penthouse.'

'And what was your vision?'

Alice thought for a moment before answering. 'I didn't really have one. Getting my registration was my next big thing, choosing an area in which to specialise. It certainly wasn't having children so soon, and definitely not on my own.'

'You'll be all right,' Jeremy said kindly, but Alice wasn't so sure.

'That's easy for you to say. The truth is, it's going to be a long, hard slog and I'll just have to make the best of it.'

'So you and Marcus are washed up? There's no chance he might reconsider when the baby comes along?'

'I doubt it. Anyway, it's entirely irrelevant how he feels. There's no way I'd go back to him after the way he's been.'

'What did your parents say?'

The flicker of pain in her eyes didn't go unnoticed by Jeremy. 'Everything Marcus did and ten times more. They really put themselves to the wall to get me through medical school—we're not really speaking at the moment.'

Jeremy gave her a sympathetic look and turned back to his meal but Alice, feeling more confident now, decided it was her turn to cross the line. 'You're still in a lot of pain from your accident, aren't you?'

Jeremy responded to her probing question in a rather

more dignified way than Alice had, but though he didn't promptly start coughing and spluttering he certainly looked suddenly uneasy.

'Has everyone noticed?'

Suddenly she felt sorry for him. He wasn't as cool as he made out. Maybe she shouldn't have mentioned it. 'No one—well, not as far as I know,' she said quickly. 'It was just that first day we started, seeing you after the clinic. I guess I realised then. And since then I've just noticed the odd couple of things, but only because I was looking. I'm sure that no one else would have.'

'I am in pain,' he said quietly. 'Not all of the time, and it certainly doesn't interfere with my work. I'd never put the patients at risk like that. But by the end of a long theatre list or the end of the day...' His voice trailed off.

'Are you taking anything for it?' she probed.

'Paracetamol—that's it. It helps a bit.'

'But not enough. Surely you could take something stronger. I mean, after all you've been through...'

'My doctor said the same, but at the end of the day I'm a surgeon. I have to have my wits about me one hundred per cent. Maybe I could take something but I have to go to my bed with my conscience. Take Lachlan Scott. It would be hard enough telling his parents if he'd died. Imagine my guilt if I'd been taking a painkiller that might have impaired my concentration.'

'But, Jeremy,' Alice reasoned, 'I'm not talking about anything mind-altering, just something a bit stronger.'

But Jeremy was resolute. 'I have to live with myself, Alice. If I need more than paracetamol to get me through then I came back too soon. I'll just have to get on with it.'

As exasperated as Alice was by his stubbornness, she also actually admired him for the stance he was taking and the personal sacrifice he was making to ensure his patients received the best of care.

'Looks like we'll both just have to lump it, doesn't it?' he said lightly.

Alice gave a small laugh. 'In my case, literally.' Raising her glass, she offered a toast. 'Here's to suffering the consequences.'

As their glasses clinked their eyes met. Again Jeremy flashed her his smile, but this time Alice didn't smile back. Her mind was suddenly in turmoil and, dumbfounded, confused, she took a hasty sip of her drink. Surely she couldn't be falling for him? Not her as well as every other female at Melbourne City?

Until that point Alice had safely assumed that your sex hormones somehow disappeared when your pregnancy test came back positive. Nothing scientifically based, of course, but for Alice it was just the way she felt. She hadn't even considered the fact she might find another man attractive. Oh, maybe somewhere a long way down the road, on the distant horizon, but it wasn't something she had dwelt on. She had enough to deal with, just concentrating on making a half-decent life for herself and the baby. But looking at Jeremy sitting across the table, immaculate, gorgeous and smiling at her, it was if she were seeing him for the first time. Suddenly he wasn't just her good-looking boss, the one with the reputation, but a man who made her laugh, who actually listened—and one with a vulnerable side, too. And for Alice it was proving to be an irresistible combination.

'What's wrong?' Jeremy asked, and Alice heard the concern in his voice.

'Nothing,' she said, flustered. 'The baby just did a huge somersault,' she lied. 'I think I'm going to give birth to a gymnast.'

'You must be exhausted. I'll get the bill.'

As he signalled the waiter Alice fished in her bag for her purse.

'Don't even think about it.' Jeremy shot her a look across the table.

'We'll go halves at least,' Alice insisted.

Jeremy seemed to find this hilarious. 'I haven't done that since I was a medical student. Anyway, that's not fair,' he joked. 'You had the steak and *two* mineral waters. Look, Alice,' Jeremy drawled. 'There have to be some compensations for spending an evening with a self-confessed male chauvinist, so at least utilise them.'

So she did. She didn't even bother to put up too much resistance when Jeremy insisted on driving her home; his leather-upholstered seats far more tempting than the tram. But as the car slid to a halt outside her block, Alice was suddenly hit by an attack of nerves.

'Er, you don't want a coffee or anything, do you?' she said, praying he would take the hint and refuse. Her poky little bedsit was hardly the Hyatt and, anyway, she couldn't remember if she'd made her bed yesterday.

But Jeremy appeared not to notice her reluctance. 'A coffee would be perfect.'

Thankfully she *had* made the bed. Jeremy instantly made himself comfortable, kicking off his shoes and flicking on the television as Alice busied herself with the coffee. Obviously strange women's apartments held no fear for him, Alice reminded herself. Luckily she had bought some filter papers at the weekend and could make a decent brew; the cheap home brand she generally survived on was definitely an acquired taste.

'I bet you hog the remote control,' Alice commented as she brought two steaming mugs through.

'Of course.'

It was a choice between the sofa or the floor, and if she sat there Alice doubted if she'd ever get up again, not in a ladylike fashion anyway, so she was left with little choice other than to sit beside him. The same feeling of awareness she had experienced in the car returned. Frantically searching for something to say, she watched as he stifled a yawn.

'You must be exhausted, too,' Alice said sympathetically. 'After all, you wouldn't have had any sleep last night with Lachlan and everything.'

Jeremy shrugged. 'Comes with the territory, though I must admit it's the first time in ages I've had to work right through.'

Alice took a sip of her coffee. 'Lucky you were on site last night and got there so quickly.' Her cheeks were burning but she couldn't stop herself. 'How come you were there?' Her grey eyes peered over the edge of her mug. Her question sounded casual enough but her heart was in her mouth as she awaited the answer.

'I was already more than a bit worried about him. I was half waiting for a call, although I admit I thought it would be from Linda. Then there's the other sickie patient we've got in Intensive Care. He's still pretty unstable. Since the accident I'm not given to speeding, as you can imagine. It seemed more sensible to stay in one of the on-call rooms when I'm on, rather than trying to make some mercy dash in the middle of the night. Safer, too.'

Even Alice was surprised at how she relieved she was that he hadn't been with a woman. OK, so who was to say that Carrie or whoever hadn't been in the on-call room with him? But at least his reasons sounded plausible.

'I don't think you fully understand how well you did last night, Alice. Cold septic shock is often terminal. We got to him just in time.'

'It's Fi you need to thank. I did nothing.'

'I've already thanked Fi. And what she said to you was right, too. It did take a lot of guts to ring me and go with your hunch. You didn't just help Lachlan last night—you made my return a whole lot easier.'

Alice gave him a bemused look. 'How?'

'As I said before, there are a lot of people watching. It would be tragic enough to lose a young fit man in any circumstances, but a fellow consultant's son...'

'No one could have blamed you, Jeremy. You did a brilliant job in Theatre, you reviewed him thoroughly postoperatively. You know better than me how subtle the signs of septic shock can be, especially in someone so young.'

Jeremy put down his empty mug. 'You're wrong, Alice. There are a lot of people waiting for me to put a foot wrong. Even if it hadn't been my fault, the consequences for me professionally would have been dire.'

'It didn't come to that,' Alice said softly.

'Thank God. Anyway, it's worked the other way, and I know that it's completely unfair on you and Fi—but I'm suddenly reaping the benefits of your wisdom. Nice as it is for now, I'm not that shallow that I don't realise it could have gone either way, and that my so-called friends slapping me on the back at the moment would have been sticking in a knife.'

'But why? Why would they want to see you brought down?'

Jeremy let out a sigh. 'Not all of them. I haven't got that many enemies. But the few I do have are pretty powerful. You know what hospitals are like, how mud sticks. I've put a few people's noses out of joint in my time, and they thought the accident was somehow my comeuppance. As you reap so shall you sow and all that.'

'Surely you can't have been that bad?'

'Of course not.' Jeremy managed a repentant grin. 'At least their daughters didn't seem to think so.'

'Ah.'

'Am I making sense now?' Those impossibly blue eyes were staring at her intently.

'Perfectly.' For a moment their eyes locked. He smiled

then, really smiled, his eyes creasing, and Alice felt her insides flip over, only this time it was definitely nothing to do with the baby.

'Can I get you another coffee?' she asked quickly, but Jeremy shook his head.

'I'd best be off.' He stood up and, smiling slightly as Alice struggled somewhat to join him from the impossibly low sofa, offered his hand, which Alice almost instinctively reached for, allowing him to take her weight as she stood up. Feeling about as seductive as a baby elephant, she managed an embarrassed laugh.

'I was fit—once. It seems like a lifetime ago.'

Jeremy grinned. 'I'm just eternally grateful it's women who have the babies.'

He made no move to go, didn't even release her hand. Instead, he stood there for a moment, his eyes searching her face. There was an unmistakable tension, but Alice assumed it was all coming from her. She was all too aware of her condition to even consider that Jeremy might reciprocate her attraction.

''Night, then, Alice.' He pulled her gently towards him and for a fleeting second his lips brushed her cheek in a casual goodnight kiss—except there was nothing casual about it for Alice. The world seemed to move in slow motion as she took in the scent of his cologne, felt his moist, warm lips graze the side of her face, her swollen stomach for a second pressing against him. It should have been no big deal, any man would have ended a pleasant evening with the same gesture, there was nothing to read into it.

But it *was* a huge deal, Alice conceded as he let her hand go. Jeremy Foster close up was every bit the exhilarating experience she had heard about. He deserved every flicker of his reputation if one tiny kiss could have that effect on a woman. No wonder they all melted, Alice reflected as he turned to leave. It would take a stronger woman than her to turn him down. 'Have a good night's sleep,' she managed to rasp.

Jeremy nodded. 'No doubt about that. I'd better book an alarm call or I doubt I'll make it.'

Alice stood there dumbfounded. 'Was it you that booked the call for me this morning?'

Jeremy gave a casual shrug. 'Sure.'

'But why?'

'I thought you needed the rest. It did Linda no harm at all to be reminded of the work an intern does. She might think she's carried the whole team for the last year, but by all accounts the only job she's been doing is mine. Everyone else had to do the rest.'

'But I told you I don't want any special treatment.' This was all too much—never had it entered her head that it might have been Jeremy who'd been so thoughtful.

Jeremy, though, seemed to think it was no big deal. 'I know you don't want any special treatment, and if it makes you feel any better I'll be sure to run you ragged tomorrow. Thirty-six hours on the go is bad enough at the best of times, Alice, let alone in your condition. You should be grabbing every opportunity to rest when you're on call.'

'Th-thanks,' she stammered.

He didn't answer. With a vague wave he opened the door and Alice stood watching as he made his way down the corridor and out through the foyer.

Walking back in, she looked at the two empty mugs side by side on the coffee-table. The scent of his cologne still hung in the air and Alice closed her eyes for a moment. Jeremy Foster was the last person she should even think of falling for. He was a flirt and a womaniser. Everything she didn't need. After Marcus, surely she had learned her lesson by now—men couldn't be trusted.

As if to prove a point, she took down a photo album from her bookshelf and opened it. Images of Marcus and

herself filled the pages. This was the man whose child she
was carrying, the man whom she'd thought had loved her,
the man she had loved. But not now, Alice thought darkly.
His abhorrent reaction to her pregnancy, his utter unwill-
ingness to stand by her through difficult times had shown
his true colours. There simply weren't any feelings of love
for Marcus left in Alice, just hurt and bitterness and an
overwhelming sense of sadness for her unborn baby.

Anyway, she concluded, snapping the album firmly shut,
she was way out of her league where Jeremy was concerned. The gossip said he liked his woman size eight, un-
opinionated and uncomplicated, and Alice failed dismally
on all three. Which was for the best really. The last thing
she needed right now was to be yet another notch on his
bedpost. Another woman in the hospital lugging around a
broken heart because she'd succumbed to his charms.
Maybe the safety of her bump could now provide a refuge
to hide behind, because Alice knew without a doubt that if
she wasn't six months pregnant it would have taken every
ounce of self-control to show Jeremy the door tonight.

CHAPTER FOUR

IF, AND for Alice it was a big if, there had been some gentle flirting going on that night, Jeremy seemed to heed her warning that she didn't want any special favours and on the work front treated her not quite as one of the boys but more or less. However, on more than one occasion she caught him staring at her, and she was almost certain that the look in those devilish blue eyes showed her that he definitely saw her as a woman. And even though Alice repeatedly told herself that she didn't want a repeat of their casual date, when she visited Josh she found herself battling with a stab of disappointment when invariably she had just missed Jeremy.

Darren Barker returned from annual leave and after a month Josh came back to work, but despite the fact that the team was fully manned for the first time in ages, the workload, like Alice's girth, only seemed to get bigger.

'Hell, what's Jeremy trying to prove?' Josh remarked when he saw the theatre list for the following week. 'There's practically a full month's worth here. Thank heavens we've got Monday off or we'd be dead on our feet. We'll never find beds for them all—they're going to have to cancel some.'

Alice didn't look up from the notes she was writing when she answered, 'No such luck. Jeremy's swung it to have some of the closed-off beds opened to get the waiting times down, so I'd make the most of this weekend if I were you. We're going to be going in all guns blazing from Tuesday. Fi's having a fit—apparently she's going to have to get a load of agency staff in, what with the new patient-staff ratios. Jeremy, in one week, is going to blow the whole year's ward budget.'

'The budget's not going to be the only thing that blows. Dianne will throw a wobbly if I keep coming home late. And, looking at this list, there's not going to be much chance of getting out on time.'

This time Alice did look up. Putting down her pen, she took a grateful sip of the tea Fi had thoughtfully placed in front of her. 'How's Dianne coping now? You said she seemed pretty down.'

Josh ran a hand through his long hair. 'I think she's just exhausted. Declan's a real live wire. It was hard enough dealing with just him, but now we've got Eamon home it's too much for her to deal with. He takes for ever to feed.' Josh leant back in his chair. 'Not that we're complaining. It was touch and go for a while, and to have him home so soon and doing so well is like having all your prayers answered at once. It's just…'

Alice, without getting up, moved her chair on its wheels nearer to Josh. 'That you're both exhausted.' She finished the sentence for him. 'Don't feel guilty for feeling this way. A sick baby is hard work at the best of times, let alone with a healthy demanding twin. It's only been six weeks. No doubt Dianne's still not caught up with her sleep, let alone everything else that's gone on. It must be hard for her, especially now you've been back at work a couple of weeks. She must be feeling pretty isolated. Have you thought of getting someone in to help?'

She watched as Josh rolled his eyes. 'I did suggest it. Dianne promptly burst into tears and said that I thought she couldn't cope and was a lousy mother. I can't win.'

'Maybe it's a bit more than exhaustion, Josh,' Alice suggested cautiously. 'Dianne could well have postnatal depression. A complicated labour, a sick baby, a multiple birth—they're all known risk factors. I should know; my obstetrician gave me a pile of leaflets to read this week. I think I'm heading for it and the baby's not even born yet.'

Josh managed a small smile at the joke. 'I think you're right, Alice. Maybe I should put my foot down and just get some help in.'

'And get her to see her GP as well. Maybe ring him and mention what it's like for Dianne at the moment. She doesn't need to know you've called, but if the GP's actively looking for signs of depression it could make diagnosis easier, and the sooner she gets help the better.'

'Thanks, Alice. I just never thought being a parent would be this hard.'

'Don't,' Alice said through gritted teeth. 'I'm starting to have a touch of stage fright.'

'Sorry.' Josh grinned. 'How long have you got now?'

'Seven weeks and counting, which means just four weeks left of this place. I must admit I'm more than ready to finish. It's getting harder and harder to roll myself out of bed in the morning. Three days off sounds just what the doctor ordered. I think we should make the most of it.'

Josh nodded. 'I intend to. Maybe I should give my mum a ring see if she can come for the weekend—take the load a bit.'

Alice pursed her lips. 'You know what they say about mothers-in-law. Another woman offering endless advice might be the straw that breaks the camel's back. I'd try breakfast in bed and lots of TLC all round, and if things don't get better, speak to the doctor. Sorry,' she added. 'I'm interfering. Your mother's probably wonderful.'

This time Josh really laughed. 'I'd say you're right again. Nice save, Alice.'

Her pager broke in and, laughing as she picked up the phone, Alice felt as if the walls had suddenly fallen in as she heard the switchboard operator's cheerful voice.

'There's a visitor for you in Reception, Dr Masters. A

Marcus Collins. Should I direct him up to the ward or would you like to come down?'

For a moment Alice couldn't speak and her mind suddenly went into overdrive. What could Marcus possibly want? What if he had changed his mind, wanted her back? Wanted to play a part in the baby's life? How would she react to that?

'I'll come down,' she managed to rasp.

'Is there a problem?' Josh asked, noticing how pale Alice had gone.

'I'm not sure yet.' Alice stood up. 'Look, Josh, I'm practically finished. I've just got one more prescription chart to write up—would you mind?'

'Sure,' Josh replied amicably. 'Alice, you'd tell me if there was something wrong, wouldn't you?'

'Anything I should know about?' Jeremy's clear tones clipped through the air and they both swung around in surprise.

'Nothing's wrong,' Alice insisted. 'An old…' She paused for a moment too long. 'Friend has just turned up. He's waiting down in Reception. I was just asking Josh if he'd mind finishing up my drug orders.'

Neither man pushed further, and Alice gratefully picked up her stethoscope from the workbench and made her way down the corridors to Reception, her heart practically in her mouth as she tried to fathom what lay ahead. But even if she'd had a full week to come up with an endless list of scenarios, never could she have envisaged what Marcus had in store.

His greeting was cool, decidedly uncomfortable even, and Alice noticed that Marcus not only couldn't meet her eyes, he was also studiously attempting to avoid looking at her hugely pregnant stomach.

'I need to talk to you, Alice.'

Alice swallowed and nodded. 'We can use one of the

pre-admission rooms.' She led him the short distance along a carpeted corridor and, after checking with the admission clerk, let them into a small admitting room, which the admissions staff used to register booked patients.

Alice sat down, her back straight, her hands folded neatly in her lap, but Marcus chose not to use the other chair, instead standing uncomfortably against the closed door as if he might make a run for it at any moment. 'What did you want to see me for, Marcus? I thought you'd said all you wanted to.' Her voice, to Alice's amazement, was cool and calm.

'There's no easy way to say this, Alice. I've met someone else and we're getting married shortly.'

Alice didn't need to worry about Marcus noticing her stunned expression. His eyes were looking everywhere but at her. Again she was amazed at her ability to keep her emotions in check. 'Well, what has that got to do with me? It's not as if you need my permission or anything.'

'I know that,' he answered irritably.

'Have you told her about me? About our baby, I mean.'

'Some of it.'

Alice stood up. She was sick of having to drag out information from him—after all, it had been Marcus that had instigated the meeting. 'Which part, Marcus? That we were together for two years and you dumped me as soon as you found out I was pregnant? Or the part where you begged me to have an abortion? Does she or does she not know that you're going to become a father in seven weeks' time? Because if the answer is no, I suggest you get a move on. Don't worry, I'm not going to come begging for maintenance, and heaven knows why I should care about how you handle yourself, but don't you think a bit of honesty might go down well at the start of a marriage?'

'I've told her all right,' he snapped. 'And Yvonne took it very well. But she is a bit worried that you might start asking for money once the baby's born. She knows first-hand how messy it can all get. She's a kindergarten teacher.'

'Which makes her an expert, does it?'

Marcus sighed. 'You have to see it from her point of view. It's hardly the ideal way to start a marriage.'

Alice was as stunned as she was sickened by his insensitivity. So stunned, in fact, it took a moment or two for his next damning sentence to sink in.

'Anyway, I've told Yvonne that if you suddenly start asking for support I'm going to insist on a DNA test, just to be sure.'

Alice grabbed at the chair-arms. 'To be sure of what?' she asked through white lips. Surely she must be mistaken? Marcus, the man she had loved, couldn't be saying this—not now, not ever!

'To be sure the baby's mine.'

Bile rose in her throat. The taste was as foul as the words she was hearing.

'Is that what you've let her think? That I was sleeping around on you?' Her voice was rising and she could feel her blood pressure hitting the roof. Stay calm, she begged herself inwardly, you've got the baby to think of. Suddenly it was all too much. 'Get out,' she shouted. 'Go on, get out.'

But Marcus made no attempt to leave. Sobbing, she rushed past him. Lunging at the door, she pulled it open, and practically ran out into the hallway—straight into the arms of Jeremy.

'Alice.' His concerned voice reached her. 'Alice, what on earth's happened?'

Shaking, sobbing, she leant against him. 'Please,' she begged. 'Tell him to go.' Jeremy's eyes travelled over her head, coming to rest on Marcus as he walked out of the room.

'Alice, we need to talk—we need to clear things up.'

'I don't think now is the time, do you?' Jeremy's voice was scathing, and if Alice had looked up she would of seen a look of pure hatred in his eyes as he distastefully eyed the other man. 'Perhaps you should do as Alice asks and go.'

For a moment it looked as if Marcus was about to argue, but something in Jeremy's stance made him think twice.

'OK, OK, I only came here to talk.' Without a backward glance he marched along the corridor and, Alice swore to herself, out of her life for good.

'I assume that was Marcus?' Jeremy said dryly, leading her back to the interview room and dragging the chair behind her. As he guided her to sit down he only just stopped himself adding that he hoped Marcus's personality wasn't heritable—now wasn't the time to lighten the mood. He pulled up another chair, sat down and put his arm back around Alice.

'Did he want to try to patch things up?' She was too overcome to hear the slight unease in Jeremy's questioning tone.

'Not exactly,' she said. 'He came to warn me off. He's getting married.'

'I'm sorry.'

Alice squinted up at him through her tears. 'That's not the problem,' she gulped. 'We've been finished for months. I never expected him to spend a year in black or anything.'

'Still, it must hurt a bit,' Jeremy ventured, but Alice shook her head resolutely.

'Surprisingly, no. Well, not much,' she admitted reluctantly. 'He said if I ask for any money he's going to insist on a DNA test.'

'Ah,' Jeremy said, his grip on her tightening somewhat. 'Someone's been talking to a solicitor.'

'Why do you say that?'

'Because that's just the sort of tactic they use, dragging things out, making everything terribly complicated when the whole world knows it's really quite straightforward.'

'But I was never even going to ask him for money. I want to support my baby myself,' Alice wailed.

'Marcus probably knows that deep down, but I'll bet it made it a hell of a lot easier telling his girlfriend there was some doubt as to whether the child was his or not than the plain truth—that he simply doesn't want to know.'

His words made sense—at least enough to stop Alice crying—and once she had calmed down it suddenly dawned on her whose arms she was in.

'How come you were here?' she asked, attempting to pull herself away, but Jeremy only held her tighter.

'Because I was concerned about you. I asked the receptionist where you had gone.'

'But why?'

'Because I was hoping she'd know and as it turned out I was right.'

This time she managed to wriggle from his arms enough to look up at him. She stared at him, nonplussed, for a second. 'I didn't mean that.'

A small smile tugged at the corner of his mouth. 'I know you didn't. All right, then, I was concerned about you because I care.'

Alice was caught completely off guard by his revelation, so much so that she sat there, open-mouthed, as he tentatively continued, 'I care a lot about you, Alice.' His face moved slowly but surely towards hers. She had every chance to move, to duck out of the way, but instead she held still. Allowing his lips to rest on hers, moving her mouth slowly against his, her hands gradually worked their way up until she could feel his silken blond hair between her fingers. The millennium fireworks were nothing on the eruptions exploding in her head as she responded to his touch.

Stunned, embarrassed, yet dizzy with desire, she sat there motionless when he finally broke away. 'Surely you've noticed?' he asked gently.

She gave the faintest shake of her head. 'No. Well, maybe the night we went out, but I thought you were just being nice…' Her voice trailed off. She was trying to look him in the eye but she couldn't tear her gaze away from his full, sensual lips. Lips that had only seconds before been on hers!

'Nice! And there I was, pulling out all the stops! What's a guy got to do to impress you, Alice?'

She could hear the humour in his words, and Alice looked up shyly. 'It never entered my head you could possibly be interested in me.'

'Why ever not?'

His question was so impossibly ludicrous that Alice gave an incredulous laugh as she spoke. 'Because I'm pregnant, Jeremy. Very pregnant, with another man's baby. It hardly puts me up there on the list of Australia's most desirable women.'

'Thank God for that,' Jeremy quipped. 'Most of them are as boring as anything and I should know—I've been out with a couple.'

The fact that she was pregnant honestly didn't seem to bother him a bit, and Alice found herself shaking her head in bemused wonder that they were even having this conversation.

'I'm sorry for losing it like that, it was just all a bit of a shock. Marcus was the last person I was expecting to see.' She was trying to make an excuse for her actions to offer him an out if that was what he wanted.

But Jeremy was having none of it. 'Don't apologise, you had every right to be upset. And I was only too happy to console you. I've got a thing for damsels in distress, in case you hadn't noticed.'

And every other female with a pulse, Alice thought cynically, trying to bring herself back to earth.

'What are you doing this weekend?'

'Nothing,' she answered without thinking, then quickly added, 'But that's deliberate on my part. I've got to see my obstetrician on Monday evening and he's told me if my blood pressure is up even a smidgen then it's maternity leave for me. I'm going to take it very easy.'

'Is there any chance Marcus might come round, hoping to resume talks?'

She hadn't thought of that!

'And even if he doesn't,' Jeremy continued, not waiting for an answer, 'you're going to spend the whole time on tenterhooks or at the very least churning yourself up by going over what he said.'

'Probably,' Alice admitted.

'Well, instead of playing Russian roulette with your blood pressure, why not come with me to Sorrento? I've got a holiday home there, on the beach. It's only about an hour or so from here, and it would be really relaxing for you. There's a nice pool and you could go for long walks on the beach.'

'No, Jeremy,' Alice said straight away. 'I really don't think it would be appropriate.' She hadn't meant to sound quite so prudish, and when Jeremy roared with laughter even Alice managed a small grin.

'On the contrary, given the fact we've finally admitted we like each other, I think it would be entirely appropriate to spend some time together.'

Alice shook her head. How could she tell him that nothing sounded more tempting than what he was suggesting, but that she felt as fat and un-sexy as she had ever felt in her life? And the thought of a weekend in close proximity with Jeremy Foster would be even worse for her blood pressure than ten visits from Marcus.

'Come on, Alice,' Jeremy insisted. 'It will do you good. I'm not asking you there so I can have my wicked way. I honestly think it will do you some good and I think it will be nice for us to get to know each other a bit better away from work. And let's face it,' he added with a wink, 'with my bad back and your huge belly I doubt we'll be rewriting the Kama Sutra!'

Once she had finally agreed to go, Jeremy seemed hell-bent on getting there. So much so he didn't even want to stop by Alice's apartment for her to pack.

'You only need a few bits and pieces—we can get them there.'

Again he just assumed either she could afford it or he would pay for her. She wasn't sure which was more annoying.

'We're stopping at my place,' she said firmly, as again Jeremy battled with her seat belt.

'Surely there must be a design fault. I'm not *that* big,' she muttered, mortified at the thought of having to go through this every time she got in his car.

Tact obviously wasn't one of Jeremy's strong points. 'You're huge, Alice,' he said without thinking, then, catching sight of her shocked expression, he quickly backtracked. 'But it's all baby,' he said hurriedly. 'From behind you wouldn't even know that you're pregnant.'

When they got to her bedsit, Jeremy stood over her as she attempted to pack.

'What do you need that for?' he asked for the hundredth time, as Alice folded the flex on her hair-dryer.

'In case I want to do some cooking! What on earth do you think I need it for?'

'Alice, we're going to Sorrento, for heaven's sake, not

Outer Mongolia! I'm sure I can rustle up a few mod cons for you. I think I can even stretch to a towel,' he said, retrieving the towel she was neatly folding and tossing it onto the bed. 'Just grab some bathers, a toothbrush and a change of clothes, and we'll be on our way.'

'Bathers? You're not serious.' She held up a stringy little bikini from her drawer. 'This is all I possess in that field and I'd probably be arrested for indecency if I wore it.' She looked at the thin straps and tiny triangles and let out a wistful sigh. 'I wonder if I'll ever be that thin again?' she said, more to herself, stuffing the bikini back into her top drawer. .

But Jeremy immediately retrieved it. 'That will be fine. Who knows, you might even come back with a tan on your stomach. You'll be the talk of the maternity ward, you scarlet woman you.'

He had this incredible ability to put her at ease, to make even the most embarrassing situation somehow amusing. He was also far too used to women jumping to his tune, Alice thought to herself as Jeremy tapped his well-shod foot impatiently. Well, he would just have to wait for her, she decided, pointedly refusing to rush as she sorted out her make-up bag. 'Before you ask what the hell I need make-up for,' she said without looking up, 'I might be the size of a house with the whitest stomach in living memory but no one, and I mean *no one*, is ever going to see me without mascara. Not even in labour.'

'You should get your eyelashes dyed; it's supposed to be marvellous. Sorry,' he added as Alice shot him a withering look. 'An ex-girlfriend of mine swore by it, and I've picked up a few tips in my time.

'So much for spontaneity,' Jeremy teased as he loaded her case into the boot a short time later and Alice made a quick dash to check for the second time that she had locked the front door. As she lowered herself into the seat, and the battle with the beastly seat belt recommenced, Jeremy caught her eye and gave her a tiny wink. 'Perhaps you should have brought that towel. You know I'd never forgive you if your waters broke on my leather seats.'

It was a point she didn't care to dwell on, but for now Alice was rather more concerned with the weekend ahead. She was having serious trouble keeping her breathing even as Jeremy slid the car into gear.

He took the beach road, the Melbourne skyline glittering orange in the rear-view mirror as they followed the long road along the bay. The views were stunning and Alice craned her neck, taking it all in.

'There's a lookout point on Oliver's Hill,' Jeremy said, glancing over. 'We'll stop there.'

Pulling in, he came round to the passenger side and helped her out. Taking her hand, he led her to the lookout point nearby. Alice caught her breath in wonder. Oliver's Hill stood behind them, the houses precariously set on its jagged slopes, their windows, designed to catch every glimpse of the magnificent bay view, sparkling in the sunset. The bay glittered before her, a magnificent horseshoe of sand and sea, with the city standing tall and resplendent on the tip, the low orange sun turning the buildings into a sparkling mass of liquid gold. She followed the curve of the beach slowly, taking in all the landmarks—Brighton, Rickets Point, Frankston Pier—right along to where they were now.

'Magical, isn't it?' Jeremy said in a low, husky voice. 'I never get tired of it.'

Alice was about to agree with him, but as he continued talking she swallowed her words, listening intently as he continued.

'After the accident, when I was discharged, my mum brought me straight to Sorrento from the rehab unit to recuperate. I don't really remember much about that time, but one thing I can recall is asking her to stop here. She didn't want to, said it would be better to head straight for the beach house, but I was adamant.' He paused for a moment. 'I can remember getting out of the car and standing right here on this exact spot, just staring, drinking it all in. It was like I was seeing it for the first time.' He turned and looked at Alice. 'I've never felt so grateful to be alive.'

The wind was whipping up around them and Alice could have, if she'd wanted to, blamed her watery eyes on that, but instead she stood there silently surveying the view, imagining Jeremy, battered and confused, and how it must have felt for him that day. How it must feel for him now. She felt privileged to be standing with him, sharing a small part of his life, the tapestry that was Jeremy. With a jolt she realised it was the first glimpse he had permitted her of his deeper side. The first time he had knowingly let the façade slip for an instant. And now she'd had a glimpse, Alice knew without a shadow of a doubt she wanted to see more.

The same way that Alice had envisaged her first child would be welcomed into the world by two loving parents, part of her had also had a vague blueprint of what pregnancy would be like. Oh, not a definite plan or a set of standards that had to be adhered to—more an assumption she would have time to focus on her child within, to revel in the changes in her body. And perhaps, more poignantly, to share the tiny yet monumental landmarks with someone who found the whole process as fascinating and wondrous as she. To date, her pregnancy had been sadly lacking in all of these. But if ever there was a time in her pregnancy when she truly felt happy, a time where her dreams were met and surpassed, it was during those precious hot summer days in Sorrento.

Jeremy had more than a few mod cons; the place was

absolutely dripping with luxuries. The huge lounge with vast white walls and dark blue leather couches was so superbly designed it was like an extension of the glittering ocean that filled the massive floor-to-ceiling windows that opened onto a huge decked area. He showed her round briefly, modestly, his only intention to ensure she felt at home. Alice didn't say anything. It was all too surreal, being here with him. But as he flicked on the light to the bathroom Alice let out an involuntary groan. It was all white, with the deepest of spas, the only splashes of colour from handpainted starfish and brightly coloured shells ingrained into the tiles, and hand-blown glass bottles.

'It's divine,' she breathed.

'Why don't you have a nice bath, then?' Jeremy suggested. 'I'm sure I can rustle up a towel from somewhere.'

Alice shot him a look as he opened one of the discreet doors, and the thickest, most luxurious towels beckoned her.

'Take your time. I'll sort out some dinner.'

There was something incredibly decadent about lying in a deep bath with bubbles up to your neck, listening to a man prepare food. Judging by the occasional crash and expletive, it wasn't something Jeremy did too often, but Alice refused her initial instinct to rush out and offer help, instead lying back and watching as the warm water lapped against her huge stomach. The baby was enjoying the sensation as much as she was and Alice gazed, fascinated, as her stomach contorted, bulging and dipping as her unborn child stretched and swooped safe within its dark, warm world. Finally, when her toes and fingers were as wrinkled as the starfish on the wall and a gorgeous scent wafted through from the kitchen, she pulled the plug and wrapped herself in a huge bathrobe.

'Better?' Jeremy enquired as she padded out into the kitchen.

'Much. I'll just go and get dressed.'

'Alice, relax. We're not at the Hyatt now; you look fine as you are.'

So she did relax, curling up on the sofa as Jeremy finished off dinner preparations.

'Something smells nice. What is it?'

'It's supposed to be a risotto.' Jeremy grimaced as he brought a laden tray over to where she sat. 'But we might have to think of another name for it by the time I'm finished. It was either that or toast. I'll have to go and do a shop tomorrow.'

Strange, Alice thought. The words 'shopping' and 'Jeremy' somehow didn't equate.

'It's delicious,' Alice uttered as she took her first mouthful. 'Funny, I never imagined you could cook so well.'

Jeremy eyebrows shot up in horror. 'Me! Cook? Rose, the housekeeper, would have dropped this into the fridge this morning. All I had to do was heat it up and warm through the bread.'

'So all that banging and crashing was you just heating it up? Jeremy, I thought you were shelling fish in there.'

Jeremy flashed her an embarrassed smile. 'I should have kept my mouth shut, shouldn't I? Anyway, I grated the Parmesan—I've got the Band-Aid on to prove it.' He held up a finger and Alice started to laugh.

They sat together on the sofa after dinner. Jeremy had opened the huge glass doors, and the darkened bay provided a magnificent backdrop. He was very easy to talk to, and she found herself opening up as she had never done, sharing with him her hopes and fears for herself and her baby.

'I just worry the baby's missing out on so much, not having a father.'

'He'll have you.'

Alice looked up. 'Or she,' she pointed out, then sighed. 'But am I enough?'

Jeremy placed his empty plate on the coffee-table. 'Of course you are. From what I've seen of Marcus—well, put it this way, I think a reluctant access visit once a month and the occasional present will screw a kid up far more than having one passionate parent who really cares.'

Alice blinked in surprise. 'It sounds like you've given it some thought.'

Jeremy shifted uncomfortably. 'I have.' He hesitated before continuing, his eyes staring out at the bay and then turning back to her. 'I've never told anyone this before, not *anyone*,' he emphasised, 'because it simply didn't seem relevant. My biological mother walked out on my father and I when I was three months old. I've never seen her since, not that I remember her from then obviously. Apart from a few photos dotted in albums, I have no idea what she's like.'

Alice couldn't keep the surprise from her voice. 'So the mother you talk about isn't your real mother?'

She could have bitten her tongue off as she watched his face darken. 'Yes, she is, Alice, in every way. Mavis is my real mother.' His features softened and Alice listened as he continued. 'She came as a nanny at first, but within a few months my father and she fell in love. They had a brilliant marriage.'

'Had?' Alice ventured.

'He died a few months ago, after I had my accident. They were the best parents anyone could ask for. Mavis was the one who got up to me at night when I was teething, saw me take my first steps, picked me up from school, helped me get through uni. It was Mavis sitting day and night beside my bed when I was in Intensive Care. Mavis is every bit my ''real'' mum.'

'But surely you must be inquisitive. I mean, don't you ever think about your real—I mean your *biological* mum?'

Jeremy shrugged. 'Not if I can help it. Sure, when I was a spotty, moody teenager, I gave Mum a bit of hard time, saying she had no right to talk to me like that, that she wasn't my real mother, but all teenagers give their parents grey hairs.'

Alice found herself smiling at the thought of Jeremy as a moody adolescent. 'So it really didn't affect you?'

'Who can tell? I'm sure I could pay a shrink a fortune to tell me that my mother's desertion is the reason I treat women so appallingly but, as I said before, that's just a load of mumbo-jumbo. The buck stops here, Alice. I had a perfectly nice childhood with two wonderful parents.'

'So why do you treat women so appallingly?' She felt the heat rise in her cheeks as she asked him, but it was something that had to be confronted. Jeremy's colourful past was something that needed to be discussed if things were ever to move further.

Slowly his eyes met hers. They were as blue and deep as the bay outside—and just as easy to drown in, Alice reminded herself. She needed a clear head for this.

'Are you sure you want to hear this?' he asked heavily, and Alice gave a small nod. 'Because I always get away with it.' He didn't say anything for a moment. 'Not a great excuse, I know, but it's the truth.'

'Have you ever been in love—I mean with any of them?'

For an age he didn't answer, but when he slowly nodded Alice felt a surge of panic. She had asked for the truth but she wasn't entirely sure she was up to hearing it. 'Just one.' He stood up and made his way over to the decking as Alice struggled up from the sofa to join him. 'And I made her life hell.'

'What was her name?' Despite her reluctance, Alice needed the details.

'Olivia,' he said softly, and Alice had to strain to hear. 'We were together five years and I mucked it all up.'

'Did you have an affair?'

Jeremy gave a low laugh but she could hear the despair in it. 'One that she knew about and one that she didn't.'

'But why, Jeremy? If you say you loved her, how could you do that?'

'Because when we were together I didn't realise that I did love her. Looking back, I actually don't think I was capable of loving anyone then. I was so into myself there wasn't room for anyone else. Anyway, when Olivia found out she promptly dumped me and made a dash for the bush. Once she'd gone I realised how much she'd meant to me. She got sick and I went after her, but it was too late. She'd met someone else by then and didn't want to know.

'Well, you'd think I'd learnt my lesson, but instead of slowing down I just went into overdrive, chatting everyone up and living life in the fast lane. "I'll show her", so to speak. Pretty immature, huh?'

'So what happened then?'

'The accident. Too tired, too fast and I nearly ended up dead. Waking up in Intensive Care and spending three months flat on your back in traction is a pretty big wake-up call. I had plenty of time to think, to realise what a jerk I'd been.'

'Did Olivia come to see you?'

Jeremy nodded. 'I thought she'd come to gloat, but she's too nice for that. She came to my father's funeral as well, and she said that all things considered, she probably knew Dad better than she knew me. She was probably right.'

Alice felt a surge of jealousy for this woman who seemed to have a claim on Jeremy's heart. 'You still loved her?' she asked, dreading the answer.

'I hardly recognised her. She looked so relaxed, so happy in herself. I then realised how much I had hurt her. I never want to feel like that again, to be the cause of so much misery.'

'If she took you back…'

'Don't go there, Alice, it's not going to happen. She's head over heels in love and probably popping out little red-headed babies now, and I'm happy for her, I really am. I may have loved her, and I still care about her, but we've both moved on. Life doesn't stay still. Sooner or later you have to get on with living, which I intend to, only this time not at the expense of other people's happiness. Hopefully I can prove to you that I've changed, if you'll give me that chance.'

Alice stood there a moment, pondering his words. She was somewhat disarmed by what he had revealed, but also touched by his honesty. It couldn't have been easy to tell it how it was, to not cover up the truth or apportion blame for his actions. She also knew they had moved on considerably, that the road they were taking in revealing so much of themselves was leading somewhere. It was a road Alice hadn't considered she would be taking for some time yet, certainly not while she was pregnant. Yet never before had she felt such an overwhelming feeling of closeness and acceptance. The fact they were attracted to each other was a given—the consequences of acting on that attraction were what terrified her.

Standing there on the decking, swamped in a bathrobe, her hair a fluffy dark cloud blowing gently in the night's breeze around her flushed face, Alice didn't look like a woman who was wrestling with the weight of indecision.

Jeremy, just inches away, was like a magnet pulling her ever nearer. His eyes seemed to be inviting her to move closer yet he never moved, leaving it for her to take that tiny but monumental leap. Slowly, hesitantly she took a step towards him. The consent in her movement was all the encouragement Jeremy needed and he held out his arms to her. Pulling Alice towards him, he held her still for a moment.

She leant against him, feeling the bulge of her baby pressing into him, his strong arms around her. Slowly his hands moved upwards and, taking her face into his hands, he kissed her slowly, deeply. Drunk on desire, she kissed him back, his thick blond hair like silk beneath her fingers, his heady scent intoxicating her senses. His kiss was all that afternoon's had been, and more. Lost in the moment, all that filled her mind was Jeremy, but it was he that pulled away, he that called a gentle halt.

'Oh, Alice.' He buried his face in her hair, breathing in deeply her soft, slightly fragrant scent. 'You don't know how good you make me feel.'

His utterances were exactly what she was thinking, and she felt the sting of tears in her eyes as she held onto him.

'What was that?' Jeremy pulled back and gave her a shocked look. 'Was that the baby kicking?'

Talk about ruining the moment!' There was nothing Alice could do but laugh as she nodded.

'I think you're right. You really are giving birth to a gymnast.' He looked down at her stomach and his hand hovered nervously over the bulge. 'Can I?'

Taking his hand, she guided it to where the baby was moving. Pressing his hand into her she held on and watched his face as he waited. Jeremy's eyes were wide with an almost childlike fascination. Perhaps sensing an audience, the baby refused to perform.

'Must have gone to sleep,' Alice murmured as Jeremy reluctantly moved his hand away.

'And so must you.' He gave her a small, gentle kiss. 'It's been a long day for you.'

He led her to her bedroom and gave her a slow, unhurried kiss goodnight. When she'd closed the door on him Alice lay on the bed and almost wept. She wanted him so badly she could never have turned him down, yet she was infinitely grateful to him for not pushing it, for giving her the chance to think before they went any further.

Of course, with Jeremy watching her like a hawk she had forgotten to pack a nightie so, slipping out of her bathrobe, Alice slipped between the cotton sheets naked, carefully placing the robe at the end of the bed. How long she lay there, staring into the darkness and listening to the waves lapping against the shore, she couldn't be sure. She was painfully, achingly aware that Jeremy lay in the room next to hers. Her lips were still stinging from the weight of his kiss, and every nerve in her body seemed to be tingling like pins and needles, as if awoken from the longest sleep and slowly coming back to life. She tried not to think of what Jeremy would be like as a lover, and failed.

To be held in those arms with nothing between them. To feel his hot skin against hers, his tongue exploring her. Stop it, she warned, trying to will herself to sleep. But sleep, the one thing she had been longing for all week, suddenly seemed inconsequential. She also badly needed to go to the bathroom—with the baby now firmly head down and growing bigger each day, Alice had a bladder with the capacity of a thimble. She tried to ignore it but to no avail. Getting up, slipping the robe back on and tiptoeing out into the dark hall, she padded about in the unfamiliar house, finally locating the bathroom. Afterwards, making as little noise as possible, she made her way to the kitchen, opened the fridge, pulled out the jug and poured a glass of water to take back to bed.

'Is everything all right?'

Hearing Jeremy's voice, she turned and smiled, the light from the fridge illuminating her features. 'Everything's fine. I just needed a drink. I'm sorry if I woke you.'

'I couldn't sleep anyway.'

'Why?' Alice asked, then blushed as she remembered the

reason for her own insomnia. But Jeremy, it seemed, had rather more practical concerns keeping him awake.

'I keep imagining you suddenly going into labour. Do I drive you to the nearest hospital or just head straight for the Women's and Children's, or do I call an ambulance?'

Alice stared at him, bemused. 'Jeremy, I'm not due for seven weeks yet. I'm sure I'll get a bit of warning. I'm not likely just to suddenly have it!'

'I know, I know.' He gave her a sheepish grin. 'I told you I'm terrified of pregnant women.'

'We're quite normal really. Come here.' She beckoned as the baby started to move. 'You might feel something now.'

This time when she placed his hand on her stomach the baby let out a hefty series of kicks, and Jeremy grinned in amazement.

'It's so strong,' he said in wonder.

Her eyes travelled over his near naked body, covered only by a small towel draped around his waist. A vivid raised scar held her gaze, out of place amongst such perfection. It looked angry and sore, and instinctively she reached out and touched it, her fingers, cool and soothing from the icy water, tracing the jagged edges of his wound.

Looking up, Alice caught her breath as he stared back at her.

'It looks sore,' she murmured.

She could feel his breath on her cheek, his bronzed skin beneath her fingers, and she knew then what she was feeling was good and right, that her love and desire for Jeremy was an entity, that something so intrinsically right could never be wrong. Slowly, she bent her head, her cool lips gently kissing the length of his scar. She heard him exhale, one hand burrowing into her hair as the other crept to her belt and struggled with the knot. She moved to help him, the gesture an affirmation for him to continue. Standing back a touch, she swallowed nervously as he loosened the robe and it slipped off her shoulders, tumbling silently onto the floor.

The rapt expression on his face dispelled the last trace of her nerves. Never in her life had she felt as sensual, as feminine. The effect of her naked body on Jeremy was bewitching. With a low moan he buried his face in her neck, his tongue cool and probing as she had known it would be as his hands skilfully explored the contours of her body until Alice thought she would faint with desire. Without an utterance they made their way to Jeremy's room, pulling back the sheet on the vast bed as he helped her down beside him.

'I want you, Alice,' he rasped. 'Tell me you want me as I want you.'

She answered him with a kiss. Hungrily her lips reached for him, their naked bodies blending together as they explored each other slowly, languorously. For Alice each stroke of his fingers, each touch of his tongue was a revelation. She had never imagined she could feel so sexually alive, so sensual, and it was Jeremy who made her feel this way. Every inch of him expressed his desire and they went on their journey of discovery together, both touchingly unsure of how they would get there but knowing they would in the end.

'I don't want to hurt you,' he said in a thick voice, his eyes like velvet as they gazed into hers. She sensed his hesitancy and knew she had to help him.

'You won't,' she murmured, slowly lowering herself onto him. They moved together, tentative at first but becoming bolder as desire and need took over. His hands cupped her glorious swollen breasts, his long fingers massaging her nipples, as ripe and tempting as summer berries. But through it all he held her with such gentleness, all the time careful, mindful of her condition, treating her with a certain reverence that further affirmed her new-found love.

Opening her eyes, she gazed down at his body beneath her. As if drawn, his eyes opened too, and she held his gaze. Their bodies joined, their eyes locked. They were one. Feeling the swell of him within her, she gave in to the sweet release, overwhelmed by throbbing intensity that seemed to ricochet through the entire length of her glistening, flushed body. And when the journey was over, as they lay together in an exhausted embrace and Jeremy pulled her closer to him, if that was possible, Alice knew that, really, the journey had only just begun.

'So that's what it feels like.'

His deep voice broke into her slumber. 'What's ''it''?' she murmured, nestling deeper into his embrace.

'Love' came the simple, heart-rending reply.

Alice lay on her side, her dark cloud of hair fanning the pillow. Tenderly he smoothed her locks and nestled his face into her shoulder, tucking his body around hers. As he snuggled in deeper one arm pulled her closer as the other held her stomach in an almost protective gesture. Despite the joy of their love-making, despite the rapture of lying here in his arms, Alice felt a tear slide down her cheek, and she realised with a jolt that the one thing she wished more than anything was that the baby inside her could have been Jeremy's.

'Alice, is anything wrong?' His voice was deep, probing, and the genuine concern she heard prohibited her from answering in case he heard the emotion in her voice. Instead she gently shook her head.

''Night, then,' he murmured into her hair, the softest of kisses sweeping her exposed shoulder. He felt her relax against him, listened as her breathing evened out, and only when he was sure she was asleep did Jeremy finally give in and let himself start to doze. Feeling the baby swooping and kicking beneath his hands, his last conscious thought as he drifted off was that he wished the child he could feel cocooned safely inside the woman he knew now he loved was his.

CHAPTER FIVE

FOR three days and nights they disappeared from the world and lived only for each other. Long hazy days, spent lying in the sun, occasionally cooling off in the huge sparkling blue pool. They only ventured out once, walking the short distance into Sorrento where they went to a fish and chip shop which Jeremy assured her was the best in the southern hemisphere. Alice found herself agreeing as they sat on the beach, squeezing lemon over their king prawns, feeding each other as lovers do. The ferry bound for Queenscliff was setting off. Alice watched as it pulled away, idly throwing the remaining chips to the rapidly gathering seagulls.

'Next time we'll take the ferry over there.' Jeremy broke into her daydream. 'There's some beautiful restaurants.'

Alice shook her head with a lazy smile. 'They couldn't beat this.'

But Jeremy begged to differ. Pushing her gently back onto the sand, he kissed her slowly, deeply, with salty lips. 'Want to bet?' he said, breaking away. 'I was about to say there's also some magnificent accommodation. We could be on our way upstairs now to a massive four-poster bed in the honeymoon suite.'

'Oh, well, in that case…'

So they ambled back, hand in hand and, though there wasn't a four-poster bed, nor a silver service restaurant downstairs, their love-making was every bit as romantic and tender as that of newly-weds. She knew there were issues to be faced; they both did. They didn't have the luxury of taking things slowly—the imminence of the baby and the fact that Jeremy was here, sharing in this precious time, spoke volumes. And though they both knew there was a lot to discuss, for this weekend at least they let the bigger picture rest, instead concentrating on each other. Their deep, emerging feelings for each other in no way compromised or conflicted with their emotions for the unborn baby. Instead, they were forging a foundation on which to build before the world rushed in and had its say.

It was Jeremy who broached the subject first.

'How's your blood pressure now?'

'Hmm?' Alice half opened her eyes as Jeremy, sitting on the sofa behind her, skilfully massaged her shoulders. 'It's probably so low Brett Halliday will admit me with *hypo*-tension.'

Alice was sitting on the floor so she didn't see Jeremy's eyes narrow, but she felt his fingers stiffen on her bare shoulders and she wriggled uncomfortably.

'Why don't you call it a day, Alice? We've got one helluva week coming up, and surely it can't be good for you, or the baby.'

It was Alice that stiffened now. 'You think I'd put the baby at risk?' She shrugged his hands off.

For the moment Jeremy tried to ignore her injured tones as he gently persisted. 'Of course not,' he said, replacing his hands and carrying on the massage. 'I know it's all happened really quickly, no one is more surprised than me how things have worked out, Alice, but I'm ready for this, I really am. I feel as if I've been waiting all my life for this moment, to be totally and utterly in love. Now, if that sounds slushy, I make no apology.' He felt her start to relax again under his touch and he carried on talking, trying desperately to win her around.

'Loving you means wanting to take care of you—all of you, Alice. I don't want you to have any trouble with your blood pressure. Of course I'm concerned about you working. I want you to be at home, putting your feet up, enjoying the last few weeks of your pregnancy. Not stuck in a hot theatre and up all night on call.'

She understood what he was saying, more than understood. As much as Alice loved her job, in the last couple of weeks that was all it had become—a job, no more than that. Something you had to do, not the labour of love it had once been. Oh, she knew her vocation would return, that she would always be, and *want* to be, a doctor, but for now she was a woman. A heavily pregnant woman who was tired and needed to rest and focus on the life within her. How easy it would be to lie back against him, to throw in the towel and let Jeremy make the decisions for her. But she had made a promise to her child, and she had also been let down badly before. There simply wasn't the luxury of choice here; she had to see it through. To hide the indecision she felt, her words came out harshly.

'So the great Mr Foster will provide? Women are actually capable of making it without a man, you know.' She swung around to face him.

'I have no doubt you're more than capable, Alice. I'm merely saying it's no longer necessary for you to work yourself into the ground—'

'You'll take care of us.' It wasn't a question, more a sneering statement, but Jeremy wasn't about to be perturbed.

'If you'll let me.'

Alice paused for a moment, gathering her thoughts. She knew her words had hurt him but she needed some time to think. It was all just happening too fast.

'I can't do that, Jeremy.' She saw a flash of pain in his eyes. 'I need us to be on equal terms. If we'd been together longer, if this were our baby…' She looked at him, perplexed. 'I'm not saying that I don't trust you, that I'm not grateful for your offer, but I've thought of nothing else but getting through my internship for over six months now. I've made plans, big plans, to move to the country, bring my baby up there… I'm not saying that I'm necessarily going to go through with them, but I need to—no, *have* to have that option up my sleeve. I can't just throw it all away on the strength of this weekend.'

'Fair enough.' Jeremy took a deep breath. 'Then how about on the strength of this? Marry me, Alice.' He paused, searching her face for a reaction, and when she didn't answer he added somewhat desperately, 'Please?'

For a second Alice couldn't quite believe what she was hearing. She knew she loved him and, despite her doubts and misgivings about men, did believe that Jeremy truly loved her, but never in a million years had she expected this. And also at the back of her mind, painfully intruding and desperately unwelcome, was a small nagging voice that warned her of Jeremy's past, his previous track record, his apparent inability to remain faithful. She needed a clear head for this, she needed absolute clarity, not the cloudy euphoria of rose-tinted glasses worn in the first giddy weeks of love. Her baby deserved that at least.

'You'd never be asking me if I wasn't pregnant.'

Jeremy looked at her thoughtfully. 'I hate to point this out, Alice, but it's not my baby. There's hardly a shotgun to my head, forcing me to do the honourable thing.'

'I know,' she conceded. A small smile tugged on the corner of her lips. 'But it is the truth. Jeremy…' She took his hands and moved her face close to his. 'I'm so grateful to you for asking me, I really am, but the timing's just not right. Ask me again when I'm thin and gorgeous and the clock's not ticking. There may not be a shotgun but we are up against the clock.'

'You're taking a raincheck, then?'

Her smile widened at his answer. 'What would you know about rainchecks, Jeremy? I'm sure you've always been able to have absolutely anything you want, when you want it.'

'Until now.'

She heard the pain in his voice and she longed to comfort him, but she wasn't going to give in. Instead she put her hands up to his face and kissed him tenderly. 'Let's just say it's on hold for now. I need to do this, Jeremy, and if we really are meant to be, we'll work it out.'

With that he had to be content.

Driving back, this time they were on the right side of the beach road to capture the full beauty of the bay. Her hand resting on Jeremy's solid thigh, Alice leant back in the seat marvelling at the sight, marvelling too at how the weekend had unfolded. She had found love, had had a marriage proposal and with Jeremy's skilful help had unleashed a sensual side to herself that she never would have believed existed. She squeezed Jeremy's thigh, as if pinching herself to make sure it was all real.

'What time's your appointment again?'

'Five-thirty.'

He glanced at the dashboard. 'We'll be there in plenty of time.'

Alice nodded. For once she wasn't nervous about her appointment with Brett. Never had she felt more relaxed or content. Surely her blood pressure must have come down?

As Jeremy slid the car into a parking spot a little later, Alice undid her seat belt.

'I shouldn't be too long.'

Jeremy nodded, 'Whatever. I'll just wait here, shall I?'

Alice hesitated. 'It's up to you.'

Jeremy shook his head. 'No, Alice, it's up to you.' She couldn't blame him for being cautious after her 'back off' speech, but she had never intended to shut him out. The fact that Jeremy wanted to be there for her, to share in this time, sealed her love even further.

'Come on, then,' she said softly.

*   *   *

'Dr Masters, I've been trying to call you.' Madge, the receptionist, replaced the receiver and gave Alice an apologetic smile. 'Brett got called away to perform an emergency Caesarean section and he's also got another woman just about to deliver, so he's had to cancel his antenatal appointments for this evening.'

It was a scenario Alice had been warned of when she had first met Brett Halliday. 'Babies come when babies come, Alice, so if I have to rush off or miss an appointment you'll have to bear with me. It will be your turn to keep a few ladies waiting one day.' Sitting there, slim, without even a trace of a bump, that day seemed a lifetime away.

'That's no problem, Madge. Should I make an appointment for next week?'

'No, Brett wants to see you weekly—he's written that quite clearly. I can squeeze you in at ten a.m. tomorrow, or there's a four o'clock appointment available on Wednesday.'

Alice pointedly didn't defer to Jeremy, and she could almost feel him bristling beside her as she said, 'Four o'clock on Wednesday will be fine. I'll see you then.'

As soon as they stepped out into the car park Jeremy turned to her. 'Why didn't you take the morning appointment?'

'Because we've got a busy day tomorrow.'

'We'd have coped. It's important to get yourself checked.'

Alice stood by the car as Jeremy unlocked it. 'And I will, but on Wednesday.'

He didn't argue the point but Alice could tell he wasn't happy. 'Look, Jeremy, if I start rushing off to antenatal appointments whenever I like, and you start treating me like a doll, people are going to start talking.'

Jeremy shrugged nonchalantly. 'Let them talk. We've

done nothing to be ashamed of.'

'I know that, but once this gets out…' She didn't know what to say. Alice could almost hear the gossip hurtling through the wards, raising questions they hadn't even answered themselves.

'You want to keep it quiet?'

Alice nodded. 'At least until my internship's finished. Surely that's for the best?'

Turning the key in the ignition, Jeremy finally nodded. 'If it makes things easier for you, that's what we'll do. But, hell, Alice, this is the one decent relationship in my life. I'm not going to act as if I'm doing something wrong.' He gave her a small smile. 'Where do you want to go?'

And though the last thing she wanted was for this magical weekend to end, Alice had a sudden urge to be at home, amongst her own familiar things.

'Do you mind if you take me home?'

Jeremy's face was crestfallen and he couldn't hide the disappointment in his voice. 'Sure.'

The journey home was tense, and suddenly Alice was filled with misgivings. What if he was regretting what had taken place? What if he was finally realising what he was letting himself in for?

Depositing her bags on the living-room floor, Alice stood uncomfortably. 'Look, I know it's not what you're used to, but I can't explain it—I just want to be at home right now. We can stay at your place another time.'

In an instant his attitude changed, his face lighting up as he broke into a wide smile. 'I thought I was dropping you off, that you wanted to be alone.'

So that explained the mood! 'Hey, you're not as cool as you make out, Mr Foster.'

'Not where you're concerned. Come here,' he said, pulling her close. 'Now that I've found you I don't ever want to spend a night apart. I'd stay in a tent if that made you happy.'

Alice leant against him. 'I don't believe a word of it. Somehow I can't imagine you without hot running water and a marble bathroom.'

'Well, maybe not a tent,' Jeremy conceded with a teasing note to his voice, 'but I hear they've come a hell of a long way in luxury caravans.'

One of the nicest aspects of falling in love, Alice mused as she listened to Jeremy singing tunelessly in the shower, was the utter joy in even the simplest of things. The pleasure of discovering the tiniest details about each other—from how they liked their coffee to the more heady details of what turned each other on. For Alice their love-making was an utter revelation. She quite simply melted at the sight of Jeremy, and had an almost insatiable desire to have him near her, touching her, unlocking secrets of her body that Alice hadn't even known existed.

Watching Jeremy walk out of the bathroom, his gorgeous masculine body ridiculous in a small pink towel, Alice let out a gurgle of laughter.

'I'm sorry. Was that the only towel you could find? I'll have to go to the laundry tonight.'

'No, you won't. You'll be far too busy tending to *my* needs to be stuck in the laundry. I'll buy some at lunchtime when I go and get a couple of shirts.'

Alice watched guiltily as he dried the collar of his Egyptian silk shirt with her hair-dryer. Only at ten last night had they realised that his suit, tie, socks and shirt were in a crumpled mess at the bottom of his suitcase.

Finally happy that his shirt was dry, Jeremy made his way over to the bed and took a grateful sip of the coffee Alice had made. Looking down, he saw her gazing at him, a dangerous glint in her eye. 'Uh-oh, no way, we'll be late,' he said as her hand reached up and grabbed the towel.

'Then you'd better be quick,' Alice said seductively, pulling him back onto the bed beside her.

It was a slightly breathless, laughing pair that eventually pulled into his reserved parking spot at the hospital. 'How am I supposed to get through the next twelve hours without touching you?' Jeremy grumbled.

'It will make tonight all the better,' Alice promised and, reaching across, gave him a long lingering kiss. 'That will have to do for now. I'll go on in—and by the way, Mr Foster, you've been a wonderful teacher. I can hardly wait for the next lesson.'

Walking across the car park, Alice could barely keep the grin off her face. Suddenly life felt good again, as if the gods were smiling on her.

'What time do you call this?' Josh gave her a friendly wink a few minutes later as Alice joined him at the sink to scrub.

'I know, I know,' Alice said, blushing. 'I missed the tram by a millisecond. Normally I'd have run for it but I'm simply not up to it.' She was saved from any further lies by the angry voice of Linda.

'About time,' she seethed. 'And, no, I don't want to hear any excuses. You know full well what sort of day we've got ahead of us. The least you could do was get here on time.'

Alice didn't answer. In truth she was only two minutes late, but ordinarily she would have been there at least half an hour ago. Seeing Jeremy walk through the door, not quite as immaculate as usual, Alice suppressed a smile. Linda's rancour was worth it.

'Morning, all.' He made no apology for being late, neither was one expected.

The team was using two theatres this morning. All the

procedures were fairly minor—hernia repairs, circumcisions and the like—but it was an extremely demanding list just by the sheer volume of patients that were being operated on.

By eight-thirty the first patient was on the table. Alice was assisting Jeremy, but once he started operating their thoughts were only for the patient.

'Mr Jacobs, thirty-two years old, with a left inguinal hernia. Today we'll be performing a keyhole repair of the bowel wall as opposed to the traditional open repair, which will hopefully mean less risk of infection and shorter recovery time. Any questions?'

Nobody answered and Jeremy began the procedure explaining his movements every step of the way. All eyes were on the screen that showed the work he was doing inside Mr Jacobs's body and Alice watched, fascinated, as the mesh that would hold the protruding bowel back in place was inserted. Jeremy made it all look so simple, operating the guides apparently effortlessly, but Alice knew that each movement took skill and patience, and though he made it look easy it certainly wasn't.

On and on they worked, the day lengthening as the list grew shorter. They stopped only for a quick coffee at mid-morning and a hasty lunchbreak.

'All right?' Jeremy asked as Alice took a bite of her egg sandwich.

'Fine,' she lied. It had been impossibly hot in the theatre and, despite sitting down, her back was absolutely killing her.

'How's things your end?' he asked as Linda marched in.

'Shipshape,' she answered briskly. 'I've sent Josh up to the ward—the workload's building up there.'

'Good idea. Alice, why don't you head up to the wards after your lunch? Linda and I will finish off the list.'

She didn't have to be asked twice.

By the time the day had ended Alice was completely exhausted. So as not to draw attention to themselves, Jeremy had left straight after the final post-operative ward round, leaving Alice and Josh to carry out his last orders. By the time she wearily climbed off the tram and let herself into the bedsit all she wanted to do was sleep. Jeremy, it seemed, had beaten her to it. Long-legged, he lay stretched out on her sofa, his feet dangling over the edge.

Alice gave him a gentle poke in the ribs. 'I thought you'd have dinner on,' she joked.

Jeremy rolled his eyes. 'I'm too exhausted to even ring out for pizza. How about we go straight to bed?'

This time when they climbed into bed it was far from Jeremy's passionate declarations of the morning. Instead they just about remembered to set the alarm before cuddling up and falling deeply asleep.

'We're like an old married couple,' Jeremy said with a laugh when they woke up. 'First time an early night's meant just that. How do you feel this morning?' he asked, after planting a soft kiss on her lips.

Alice winced as she opened her eyes. A thumping headache wasn't the best way to start a day and night on call.

As Jeremy wandered off to make the coffee she lay there for a moment. Just three weeks or so to go. It sounded such a short time but it seemed like an eternity. If Jeremy asked her now to chuck it all in she'd be hard-pressed to refuse. Shaking her head ruefully, she headed for the shower. It was simply a question of mind over matter, she insisted to herself. She wasn't about to give in now.

Jeremy might have got the waiting lists down a fraction but there was definitely a down side to his surgical vigour. The ward round was interminably long, not helped by the fact that Jeremy and Josh had already been summoned to Theatre to perform an urgent laparotomy on a road trauma victim. Which left Alice to do the round with Linda, whose venom seemed to have taken on a stronger bite this morning. Every patient, it seemed, needed an inordinate number of tests or changes to their drugs or IV regimes, which all fell on Alice.

'Well, that was pleasant.'

Fi's sarcasm didn't go unnoticed as the two women watched Linda depart through the ward doors. 'I'd love to give you a hand, Alice, but I'm snowed under myself. Half the staff are agency this morning. Luckily they all seem excellent nurses, but half my day's going to be spent showing them where things are kept.' She gave an apologetic smile.

'I'll get there, Fi,' Alice said gloomily, staring at her long list of jobs.

And she would get there, Alice decided, if her pager didn't go off every five minutes or the nurses didn't keep asking her to write up drug orders that really could have waited.

'Er, Doctor, I've just started to do Mr Linton's dressing and I think you ought to take a look.' A young nurse Alice didn't recognise hovered nervously.

With a sigh Alice made her way over to Mr Linton's bedside.

'It's looking a bit red around the edges,' the nurse commented as she peeled back the sterile drape she had placed over it.

'I already saw it in the ward round, and it hasn't changed since then,' Alice said, trying to keep her voice even. 'Miss McFarlane's instructions were to start him on IV antibiotics and to clean the wound and apply a dry dressing.'

'But there's nothing in the notes or on the drug chart.'

Alice sucked in her cheeks. 'If you'd give me a moment alone, maybe I could get around to writing up some notes and charts.' And, turning on her heel, she brushed through the curtains.

'Damn,' she cursed through gritted teeth as she sat down at the workstation. Taking her frustration out on the poor agency nurse had made her feel no better. It wasn't the nurse's fault—she was right to be concerned about the wound. If only Josh were around, maybe they could get up to date. Massaging her temples in an effort to quell the throbbing in her head, Alice picked up her pen and started writing.

'There's a new admission up from A and E,' Fi said brightly, as a trolley carrying an elderly lady whizzed past. 'Apparently Linda wants her clerked straight away so we can commence the IV antibiotics.'

'Great,' Alice muttered under her breath.

The patient was a varicose leg ulcer. Mrs Dalton was a diabetic and her poor circulation made her prone to this type of difficulty. Even the smallest wound could create a problem for patients like her, and in this instance her ulcer had shown no improvement, even though she'd had twice-daily visits from the district nurse. Now, despite the nurse's diligence, it had become infected.

'I'm sorry, Mrs Dalton, I know you've been through this already, but I'm going to need to examine you and ask a few questions.'

'No worries, love, I know how it all works. Well, I should by now,' she joked, gesturing to the huge pile of old notes Fi had thrust at Alice.

'How long have you been a diabetic?' Alice asked as she gently lifted the sterile drape with which the nurses had covered the ulcer.

'Since I was ten.'

'So no doubt you could tell me a thing or three about it?'

Mrs Dalton laughed. 'No doubt. You ask away, love, I'm

a mine of information. At least you don't think you know it all, not like that madam I saw before. What was her name?'

Alice took a leaf from Jeremy's book and simply evaded the question. 'It looks very painful.'

'It is. Sarah, the district nurse, said you might order a needle for me before I have it changed. Normally I don't like taking anything but, 'struth, if you knew what it felt like when they start prodding and poking it. I'm not one for whingeing normally...'

Alice gave a sympathetic smile. Mrs Dalton had the tough, sun-battered face of a real Aussie battler, and from the brief look she'd had of her notes Mrs Dalton definitely wasn't a 'whinger'—she had put up with a lot from her diabetes.

'I'll write you up for something strong and the nurses will give it to you before they do your dressing.'

Even though Mrs Dalton had only come in for dressings and IV antibiotics, Alice still had to examine her patient thoroughly and take a detailed history. Her head was pounding and tiny little dots seemed to be dancing before her eyes as she wrote her notes. By the time she had finished the clock was edging towards twelve and her body, tired before the day had even begun, now ached mercilessly for its bed, yet she still had the rest of the day and night to get through. It was in that instant Alice knew she simply couldn't do it any more. Enough was enough.

The dots on the page blurred as tears filled her eyes. The sound of Fi's gentle voice came as no surprise.

'How about we take five in my office?'

Gulping, Alice nodded gratefully and followed Fi like a child. Fi let her cry for a moment before she spoke.

'Not having the best day, huh?'

'How did you guess?' Alice said, half laughing at herself.

'Well, when the agency nurse said a female doctor had

snapped at her, of course I assumed it was Linda. But when the same nurse put it down to hormones I did a double take. We all know Linda hasn't got any.'

Alice gave a small laugh, then started crying again. 'I've got this terrible headache. I thought it was because I was tired, but now I'm starting to get little spots in front of my eyes.'

Fi's expression changed abruptly. 'Since when?'

'Just in the last five minutes or so.'

Fi's slim delicate hands picked up Alice's. 'Your fingers are swollen—not much, but they definitely are. Have you had your blood pressure checked recently?'

'I've got an appointment at four. It's not been too great at the best of times.'

Fi tutted. 'You silly girl,' she said, but not unkindly. 'What on earth are you doing here?'

'I'm beginning to wonder myself.'

Fi took over. She disappeared, returning with a blood-pressure machine. Now, let's see what your blood pressure's doing.' She wrapped the cuff around Alice's arm. Feeling it tighten, Alice sat there, resigned. As Fi pumped it up even higher Alice felt in that moment all her dreams evaporate.

'How high?' she asked when Fi had finished.

Fi didn't answer straight away. 'I think you ought to ring your obstetrician.'

'How high, Fi?' Alice demanded, her voice urgent.

'One hundred and sixty over a hundred.'

And suddenly work, her internship, the GP rotation all paled into insignificance. Both she and the baby were in real danger.

'I thought I might find you in here! When you can drag yourself away from your morning coffee, there are a few patients that need to be seen.'

Alice didn't bother to look up as Linda rattled on. It was

Fi who spoke, her voice clear and calm, but Alice recognised the note of urgency health professionals reverted to when there was a real problem. 'Dr Masters isn't feeling well, Miss McFarlane. I've checked her blood pressure and she needs to go to her obstetrician *now*.'

Alice heard the subtle shift in tone on the last word.

Suddenly Linda was all concern. 'Why on earth didn't you say something, Alice?' She came over. 'Who's your obstetrician?'

'Brett Halliday.'

Linda nodded. 'I know him well. Look, do you want me to arrange transport to the Women's and Children's?'

Alice shook her head vehemently 'I'll take a taxi.'

'Nonsense,' interrupted Fi. 'I'll drive you. I'm due for a lunchbreak. Rowena Sheldon's an associate charge nurse. She can manage for half an hour while I take you.'

Alice nodded gratefully.

'That settles it, then,' Linda said efficiently. 'I'll ring Brett and tell him you're on your way. I'll let Jeremy know. Don't worry about a thing.'

As Alice handed over her pagers to Linda she knew without a shadow of a doubt she wouldn't be back; she wouldn't even be going back to her flat. The next time she came home it would be, God willing, with her baby.

Alice was infinitely grateful for Brett Halliday's professional unruffled manner. He examined her thoroughly, listening to the baby's heartbeat and checking her urine and blood pressure.

'You know I'm going to admit you, don't you?' he asked as Alice lay back on his examination couch. His hand was feeling her fundus—the top of her uterus—to check the size of the baby. Without waiting for her to answer, he continued, 'Your blood pressure's still up, you've got mild fluid retention and there's protein in your urine. Any one of these can happen, but combined in pregnancy we have to tread cautiously.'

'It's my fault, isn't it?'' she said, fighting back tears, but Brett wasn't about to apportion blame.

'Pre-eclampsia is also referred to as the disease of theories. No one can pinpoint exactly why certain women develop it. Yes, you've been working hard, and with your blood pressure a bit high, which you know was a concern, but healthy stay-at-home mums also develop it. The important thing now is to bring your blood pressure down and help you get as much rest as possible. Hopefully that will halt the progress of it.'

'But what if it carries on? What will happen to the baby?'

'Let's take it a step at a time, shall we? For now we'll get you admitted. The midwives will put you on the CTG monitor at regular intervals to keep an eye on the baby, and I'll arrange an urgent ultrasound and cord studies. If there's any signs the baby's in distress or it isn't receiving adequate nourishment we'll be straight onto it.'

'But it's too soon. I'm only thirty-four weeks.'

Brett squeezed her shoulder reassuringly. 'Let's do the ultrasound, shall we?'

Settled into bed, Alice tried vainly to calm herself down, but to no avail. Everything Brett had said she understood, but she felt as guilty as hell—and not just because she'd continued to work. A little voice inside her warned that this was payback. If she hadn't swanned off for the weekend with Jeremy, hadn't spent the time making energetic love, none of this would have happened. It never entered her head that, had Jeremy not intervened when Marcus had confronted her on Friday, she could have been in exactly this situation, only five days sooner. That lying by the pool, being massaged, fed and pampered by the man she loved, could possibly have kept her blood pressure down.

Her self-imposed guilt only deepened when Brett returned to her bedside with the ultrasound results.

'I won't beat around the bush, Alice. The baby's not in any distress but your placenta's not functioning as well as it should, and it's not going to provide adequate nutrition to carry the baby to term.'

'Which means…'

'You'll be having the baby sooner rather than later.' He gave her a gentle, reassuring smile. 'We'll see if we can get you to thirty-six weeks. But even if you have the baby now, it's still a good size, though it will mean a stay in special care. We're going to start you on steroids, which will help to develop the baby's lungs. The most important thing you can do for your baby and yourself is to try not to worry. I know I'm asking the impossible but it really is imperative that you try and rest and eat well. Hopefully we can add a few grams to the baby's birth weight. Now, I know you don't want to get in touch with the baby's father, but is there anyone else we can get in to be with you? You should have some support—what about your parents? I'm sure if they were aware of the circumstances they'd be ready to patch things up.'

Alice shook her head. 'I'm not up to one of my mother's lectures. Honestly, Brett, it really wouldn't help at the moment.'

'Some friends, then?'

Alice thought of her loyal friends back in Adelaide. Jess would come at the drop of a hat if she called her, but it was hardly fair. Like herself, Jess was at the end of her internship.

'There is someone,' she said quietly, thinking of Jeremy. 'He'll probably be here soon.'

'Good.' Brett uncharacteristically patted her arm. 'Now, I've written you up for some sedatives. Nothing too strong,' he added, noting her alarmed expression. 'And before you ask, no, it won't harm the baby—that's what we're trying to prevent. Remember, we're all batting for the same team here. They'll just help you relax and, as I said before, that's crucial at this stage.' He smiled as a young nurse entered with a plastic medicine cup. Grumbling, Alice swallowed the small pill.

'Are you going to check under my tongue?'' she asked as Brett stood there, making sure she took it.

'I'm sure it's not necessary.'

'Giving you a hard time, is she?' Alice almost started crying again as there in the doorway, paler than usual and slightly breathless, stood Jeremy.

Brett Halliday obviously recognised him and immediately walked over and shook his hand. 'G'day, there, Jeremy. I was just telling your young intern here to lie back and stop worrying. I hope you're not going to undo all my hard work. She feels bad enough as it is about stopping work.' Brett spoke in a light, jovial manner but again Alice could hear the coded undercurrent that warned all was not well.

Jeremy obviously heard it too. 'Don't worry, I'm not here to talk shop. I just wanted to see how she was doing.' Walking over to the bed, he looked down at her. 'Linda only just told me. I came as soon as I heard.'

Alice saw a flash of confusion pass over Brett's usually impassive features, but he didn't say anything and quietly left.

Once they were alone Jeremy sat gingerly on the bed, picking up her swollen hand. 'What happened?' he asked, his voice thick with concern.

She so badly wanted to be angry with him, to somehow offload her guilt and blame him for all of this, but, looking into his worried blue eyes, she knew he didn't deserve it. 'I've got pre-eclampsia. My blood pressure's through the roof. And Brett just told me the baby's likely to be born sooner rather than later.'

'It will be all right,' he said confidently, but it wasn't what she needed to hear. Angrily she pulled her hand away.

'How would you know?'

Jeremy gave a helpless shrug. 'Because it has to be,' he said simply. As her face dissolved into a mass of tears he pulled her into his arms, holding her close as she sobbed onto his chest. 'It has to be,' he said again, closing his eyes in a silent prayer.

CHAPTER SIX

ALICE did her best not to worry. She took the tiny yellow pills and read endless magazines until the words blurred in front of her and she drifted off to sleep. She ate all the meals that were placed in front of her and only got up to go to the toilet and have a brief shower in the morning. She didn't even have to feel guilty about letting them down at work as Josh and Jeremy both told her that her position had been immediately filled by a young overseas doctor named Mai Wing. But, despite the best medical care and the most compliant of patients, nothing was going to prolong this pregnancy beyond thirty-five weeks.

'You've had a few days' worth of the steroids,' Brett said gently as he broke the news late on Monday evening. 'All the indications are that the baby will do well. Now, as it won't have the last few weeks *in utero* it won't have laid down any fat reserves so you can expect it to be quite scrawny. Also, he's going to need a lot of small, frequent feeds, which will exhaust him—'

'It's a boy, then?' Alice asked, jumping on Brett's words.

'Force of habit,' he assured her, but Alice was convinced now she was having a son.

'Just wait and see, huh? Now, I know you're keen to have a natural birth and we're going to give you a small trial of labour, but any signs that you or the baby aren't coping and I'll do a Caesarean section without question. You understand that, don't you?'

Alice nodded.

'Good. Right, then, I'll see you in the morning. Enjoy

your sleep—it's the last good one you'll be getting for a while.'

Lying back on the pillow, Alice put a shaking hand down to her stomach. 'It's all right, baby, you'll be here beside me tomorrow. Try and rest now.' Closing her eyes, she tried to think positive thoughts to stay calm, sure the baby would pick up on the utter fear she was feeling. She was concentrating so hard on the baby that it took a moment of two to register that someone had come into the room. Opening her eyes, she gave a trembling smile to Jeremy. 'All systems go tomorrow.'

He heard the break in her voice and in a second he was on the bed beside her.

'I know you hate me saying it, but things really are going to be fine. You've done very well to get this far.'

Gulping, she nodded. 'Do you really think so?'

'I know so. That extra week will have made all the difference to the baby, you know that as well as I do. It's time now, Alice. At least once it's here you can feed it up. *Everything* really is going to be all right.'

Alice lay back on the pillow. He sounded so sure she almost believed him.

'Now…' He squeezed her hand. 'About tomorrow. I know it's all happened quickly, and I know you want to wait before we make a commitment, but would it help if I was there for you tomorrow?'

Alice gazed over at him, taking in the deep blue eyes, the full mouth that had touched hers. She wanted him there more than anything, didn't want to do this alone, but it was such a huge thing to ask, such a big step in the direction of commitment.

Jeremy seemed to read her mind. 'It doesn't have to mean anything's written in stone. I've been to the medical library and borrowed all the trendy labour books.' He held up a bulging carrier bag. 'It's almost old hat to have a husband there these days—I'd be called your "support person". Apparently we're supposed to draw up a list of your wishes and desires throughout labour and if you start to stray from your chosen course I'm supposed to step in.'

His superior dry teasing tones bought a smile to Alice's lips.

'Personally I'd be screaming for all the drugs available—perhaps I shouldn't have looked at the pictures.'

Alice really laughed now. 'It will be a bit more graphic than a few textbooks tomorrow,' she warned.

'I'll stay at the head end of the bed, I think, shouting instructions from the sidelines, so to speak. That is, if you want me there.' He looked over to her almost shyly, and Alice knew it would have taken a lot for him to ask. She could almost feel the tension in the air as he awaited her decision—it evaporated as she gave a nod.

'It would mean a lot to me…'

Jeremy swept her words away and planted a brief kiss on her cheek. 'Now, you, young lady, ought to get some sleep, and I'm off home to do some reading. Did you know that in some cultures they actually eat the placenta afterwards? I think we'll skip that part and settle for a bottle of Moët.'

'Jeremy…'

He turned in the doorway.

'You'll make sure I stay presentable, won't you? I mean, I'm not into baring all in front of everyone.'

'I hadn't noticed,' he quipped, then, seeing her anxiety, he stopped the jokes.

'Leave it with me.'

As he left Alice couldn't wipe the smile from her face. He always did this to her, somehow managed to cheer her up, make her load seem a little lighter. And tomorrow he was going to be there with her every step of the way.

When the night nurse came in to check Alice's prescription chart and her IV site, half expecting to find her in floods of tears, she was pleasantly surprised to find Alice in the deepest of sleeps, her hair fluffed out over the pillow, a ghost of a smile on her lips.

'What a beautiful day to have a baby.' Bridgette, the midwife, flung back the curtains as Alice sat up slowly, blinking in surprise.

'Goodness, I did sleep well.'

'Now, I'm just going to do your obs and then you can have a shower. Do you want to wear your own nightdress or one of our gowns?'

Alice took the white hospital gown Bridgette was offering.

'Good choice. Right, I'll be back in fifteen minutes or so,' she said, after checking Alice's temperature and blood pressure and listening to the foetal heart on the small Doppler machine. 'Do you want to ring your mum again?' she asked gesturing to the phone.

Alice shook her head. 'She wasn't particularly inspiring when I called her last night. I think I'll wait till it's over.'

'Second good choice of the morning,' Bridgette said enthusiastically. 'Surround yourself with positive vibes.'

'Are you going to be with me this morning?' Alice asked, trying not to sound anxious.

Bridgette came back from the door and enveloped Alice in the biggest of hugs. 'I wouldn't miss it for the world. Now, do you have any favourite oils you'd like me to burn?'

Alice shook her head dumbly.

'Good. That means I can choose. You enjoy your shower.'

Alice smiled as Bridgette left. Normally the most untactile person, Alice was surprisingly comforted by this slightly eccentric woman. Many nights she had sat on the edge of Alice's bed and told her how she'd 'surfed the menopausal internet' and had discovered massage and aromatherapy, convinced it had calmed her raging hot flushes and palpitations. As a doctor Alice was somewhat sceptical, but Bridgette was so utterly convinced and delightfully wacky, yet still completely assured and professional, that Alice felt soothed immeasurably that it was Bridgette who would be with her during this most special of times.

After she'd showered, Bridgette took her down to the delivery suite and showed her around.

'In the first stages you can wander around. Here's the television room, but don't have anything to eat or drink. Some mums have a bath but as Brett will probably rupture your membranes we'd rather you didn't have one; you can always have another shower.'

Alice took it all in, eyeing everything nervously. Her medical training seemed to have flown out of the window and she felt a complete novice.

'We'll monitor you and the baby regularly throughout, but try and be as mobile as possible in the early stages— it helps speed things along. Here's Brett now.'

Brett was as kind and efficient as ever. 'OK, then, Alice, we're going to start you on a small dose of Syntocinon. We can always increase it if needed, but we don't want to start the contractions off too violently, especially with the baby being a bit on the small side.'

Alice watched as he checked the dosage with Bridgette and the IV infusion was connected to the bung in her arm. 'Now I'm going to rupture your membranes. It won't hurt, just be a bit uncomfortable.'

As Alice lay back through the procedure she did her best to relax and try not to feel too embarrassed. Brett would have done this a thousand times before but, still, it was most undignified. Through it all Bridgette held her hand reassuringly.

'There, now, we'll just attach you to the CTG monitor for a short while to check how the baby's doing, and then you can get up and have a wander. I'll be in to check on you a bit later.'

Bridgette stayed after he had left. 'Baby's looking fine. I'm just popping out for five—here's the call bell if you need anything.'

She returned a moment later. 'Here's Jeremy.'

'Are you decent?' His haughty tones filled the room as he breezed in, carrying a bundle of newspapers.

'For now.' Alice answered. 'You seem set for a relaxing morning,' she said, eyeing the newspapers.

'I hope so. It's not every Tuesday I get the day off.'

Alice pursed her lips and tried not to show her disappointment.

Ruffling her hair, he started to laugh. 'I thought you might like to keep them for the baby as a momento.'

'Oh,' Alice gasped. 'How nice of you. Thank you,' she managed, instantly mollified.

She had read the same books as Jeremy and both, despite their medical training, were somewhat deflated to find that Alice wasn't suddenly thrown violently into overwhelming contractions. Her confidence ebbing as the minutes ticked by, she agreed to Bridgette's suggestion that they go for a wander. Ever the gentleman, Jeremy guided her IV pole, making sure it didn't overbalance with the weight of the IVAC pump that carefully regulated the medication Alice was receiving. Alice waddled alongside him, her slippered feet not making a sound on the highly polished floor. They didn't wander far as there really weren't a lot of options. Alice peered through the theatre doors, watching as the midwives—identified by their floral paper caps—bustled along.

'Don't even look—that's one corridor you're definitely not going down today.'

'I hope not,' Alice replied nervously.

They settled in the TV room. Jeremy refused a drink at first, but when Alice assured him that she didn't feel like one anyway he eventually succumbed and made himself a coffee as Alice pretended to watch *Good Morning, Australia*.

Watching Jeremy, long-limbed in designer blue jeans and a casual polo shirt, she felt she had to pinch herself. She still found it hard to believe that he was really here with her. A small sigh escaped her lips and Jeremy was instantly by her side, the coffee forgotten.

'Anything?' he asked anxiously.

'I'm not sure,' she lied. She was saved from further explanation by Bridgette breezing in.

'Only me.' After checking Alice's blood pressure, Bridgette gave her shoulder a reassuring squeeze. 'If only your blood pressure had behaved as well as it's doing today, huh?' Discreetly moving the gown, she squirted some jelly on Alice's abdomen and listened for the heartbeat with the Doppler. 'Everything's fine.'

Alice caught her breath. A tightening in her stomach seemed to be intensifying. Bridgette didn't say anything but calmly held her hand on Alice's bulge until the tightening eased off.

'Things are starting to happen,' she said brightly. 'I'll leave you two to it.'

Trying to concentrate on the cookery demonstration taking place on the screen, Alice found she was rocking in the chair as the tightening intensified, and Alice found herself suddenly irritated by the noise of the television. Jeremy, seemingly relaxed, laughed as the TV host made one of his usual jokes.

'Turn it off, would you?' she barked uncharacteristically.

Jeremy knew better than to argue and immediately

flicked off the screen. 'If I'm taking up too much of your time?' Alice snapped.

Suddenly it wasn't tightenings that she was having, it was definitely pain. Alice started to rock harder in the chair.

'Can I do anything?' Jeremy asked. 'Should I get someone?'

'Just talk to me, instead of watching the damn television,' she demanded.

'I think we ought to head back to the room, Alice,' Jeremy suggested, and something in his voice told her he wasn't to be argued with.

Surprisingly obedient, she allowed him to help her stand, unaware that he had pushed the call bell.

'Everything all right?' Bridgette appeared in the doorway.

'It would seem the TV's not the thing Alice wants to see right now!' Jeremy said sweetly, but Alice was sure he was raising his eyebrows at Bridgette.

'Oh, can you all just shut up?'

Without a word Bridgette led her back to the delivery suite and helped her onto the bed. 'Now, young lady, how about I do a quick internal…'

Bridgette was still smiling hours later as she came to the head of the bed and Jeremy swiftly arranged the sheet after another internal. 'What a clever girl. You're seven centimetres dilated.'

'Can I have some drugs now?' Alice gasped as another contraction gripped her. Jeremy held her against him and, guided by Bridgette, placed the ball of his fist into the bottom of Alice's back, applying firm pressure. As the pain abated Alice listened in horror as Bridgette gently explained she was too far gone for pethidine.

'By the time the drug took effect it would be useless

anyway. Keep going with the gas—it won't be too long now.'

The expletive that escaped from Alice's lips didn't seem to remotely bother Bridgette but Jeremy looked at Alice, stunned. 'She doesn't mean it,' he gasped. 'She's the most gentle, dignified—'

Bridgette cut off his excuses with a friendly wink. 'They're always the worst.'

From there on it was sheer and utter hard work. Alice sucked furiously on the gas, at times throwing it across the room in frustration, only to beg to have it back. Through it all Jeremy was beside her, slightly bemused but with an endless line of chatter that served to placate and irritate with alarming irregularity. He gave up trying to replace the sheet for the hundredth time when Alice stripped off her gown and demanded to stand. And suddenly he was behind her, taking her weight as he held her arms and she leant against him in a semi-squat. The urge to push was a wonderful relief, an almost primal instinct. No longer was the pain overwhelming her with nowhere to go. Suddenly there was something she could do. Bearing down, she grunted and gasped, pushing harder and longer as Jeremy and Bridgette urged and cheered her on. The sight of Brett tying an apron was the most welcome sight she could imagine.

'How much longer?' she gasped.

Brett gave her a steadying smile. 'That's up to you, Alice. The harder you push the sooner your baby will be here.'

It was all the incentive she needed. Suddenly an end was in sight, and with Jeremy murmuring words of encouragement, a life jacket in the stormy ocean, Alice could see land.

'Come on, Alice, one big push now—come on, Alice.' She could hear Brett's voice urging her on.

'Come on, sweetheart, I'm so proud of you. Push, Alice, one more, come on,' Jeremy urged.

And when she could push no more, when it all seemed utterly too much hard work, suddenly Bridgette exclaimed, 'Your baby's got black hair—feel it.'

Feeling the silken hair, knowing her baby was nearly out, was all the incentive Alice needed. Purple in the face, Alice took a deep breath, pushing harder and longer than seemed humanly possible. Suddenly, and far more quickly than she had imagined, a slippery bundle was being thrust into her arms, and Jeremy was gently lowering them onto the huge beanbag behind her.

Stunned, rapt, utterly shell-shocked, she gazed in wonder at the tiny angry bundle in her arms, watching as the denim blue colour of her baby almost instantaneously changed to a healthy pink, like litmus paper dipped in acid, and furious squeals of indignation poured from its wide open mouth.

'As he was so wonderful, shall we let Jeremy do the honours?'

Bridgette held up the scissors and Alice nodded, watching as Jeremy's normally steady surgeon's hand trembled with the sheer emotion of the moment when he severed the umbilical cord, tears streaming down his face.

'She's so beautiful,' he murmured.

'A girl?' Alice gasped. 'I've got a daughter? Hello, darling, hello, beautiful girl,' she crooned she held the slippery pink body to her naked breasts. 'Welcome to the world, little lady.'

Once the final stage of labour was over, and the placenta safely delivered, they had some time alone, the three of them, exploring the ten tiny fingers and toes, the sweet rosebud mouth, and the dark locks plastered to the baby's head, with the creamy vernix that had protected her inside her mother. And all the time Jeremy whispered words of endearment, telling her over and over how wonderful she had been, how proud he was to have witnessed this miracle. Bridgette joined them again, her eyes welling with tears. The wonder of birth never failed to touch her, no matter how many times she was privileged to share it.

'How about we give her a bath now?'

Normally it could have waited until Alice was more ready, but the babe was rather small and needed some warm clothes and rest, so the first bath was left to Bridgette as Alice sat shakily on a chair beside the sink, with Jeremy crooning beside her. The tiny nightie Alice had brought seemed to swamp the infant, and when Bridgette produced a lemon woolly beanie and popped it on the baby's head Alice realised for the first time just how small her baby was.

A Perspex crib was wheeled beside Alice's bed and they watched as Bridgette deftly tucked her in then placed an overhead heater above the crib. 'Just to help with her temperature, but the paediatrician's very happy with her and said she can stay beside you for now—though we'll bring her into the nursery tonight to let you rest and to keep an eye on her.'

Alice couldn't take her eyes off her. 'Can I get her out a bit later?'

Bridgette nodded reassuringly. 'Of course you can. We'll let her rest for now, though. You, too, Alice—you're probably exhausted. Have you thought of a name?'

'Maisy,' Alice murmured, looking over at her sleeping baby. 'Maisy,' she repeated, her eyes darting to Jeremy. 'Do you like it?'

She watched a smile steal across his face as he gently repeated the name. 'I think it's beautiful.' Walking over to the crib, he gently stroked the tiny soft cheek. 'Hello, little Maisy,' he whispered, and Alice thought her heart would burst.

*　　*　　*

After what felt like the longest, most important day of her life, Alice awoke from a deep sleep. Her eyes instantly focussed on the crib beside her and her heart beat faster as she realised it was empty. Turning slightly, she saw Jeremy silhouetted at the window, a swag of blankets in his arms, whispering baby talk to her precious daughter.

'Is she awake?'

'Wide awake,' he said softly, and, making his way over, he gently placed Maisy into her mother's arms. 'She smiled, Alice, I swear. I was showing her the moon and the stars and she smiled.'

Alice gave an indulgent smile as she held her newborn close. 'I don't think they smile this early, Jeremy, it was probably just wind.'

She looked up, holding his gaze as he moved closer on the bed, his strong hands gently reaching out for both of them. 'Thank you Jeremy, for being there today.' Her voice was shaking with emotion and the words seemed a paltry offering for the gratitude she felt, but Jeremy swept her words away.

'It's me that should be thanking you, Alice, for *letting* me be there.' He glanced down at the tiny babe. 'I wouldn't have missed this for the world.'

CHAPTER SEVEN

PHYSICIAN, heal thyself. Alice had heard the old saying a hundred times but, just as most doctors did, she ignored her increasingly obvious symptoms as she struggled on in those hormonal, exhausting postnatal days. As Josh had before her, she ignored signs most doctors would have seen at a glance if only they hadn't applied to them. A difficult pregnancy, lack of support, financial problems, custody issues, a difficult baby all pointed to an increased susceptibility to postnatal depression.

It was probably unfair to call Maisy a difficult baby, when really she was the most sweet-natured little thing. But the lack of those precious last weeks *in utero* meant that for now she needed strict two-hourly feeds, and the sight of her tiny body with a little woollen beanie tore at Alice's heart. The doubts and angsts that had plagued Alice before Maisy's birth seemed to have resurfaced and multiplied at an alarming rate, and the fact she was having great trouble with her milk didn't help matters. She felt that she had failed Maisy more than once and that breastfeeding was her chance to rectify this, but it wasn't to be.

'How are my two beautiful girls?' Jeremy breezed in, immaculate as usual, and Alice lay there defeated after yet another unsuccessful attempt at feeding Maisy, all too aware of her unwashed hair and shiny puffy face. 'I stopped by your flat and picked up your post as you asked. Here.' He placed a pile of letters on her bed. 'And I even cleaned out the fridge. Just as well I carry some latex gloves in the car—there were a few science experiments going on.'

'You didn't have to do that.' Alice gritted her teeth. 'I'll be home tomorrow. I could have sorted it out then.'

'It was no trouble,' Jeremy said airily, deliberately ignoring the tense note in her voice. 'Have you had any visitors?'

Alice shrugged as she flicked through her post then wearily placed it in her locker. She didn't have to open them to know they were all bills. 'Josh dropped by, and Fi, and a couple of other colleagues.'

'Your mum didn't come, then?' he asked gently.

'Well, it's hardly a five-minute car journey; it's over an hour's flight from Adelaide,' she said defensively. 'And it's not as if the flat's the most luxurious of accommodation. She'll probably come over once I'm home.'

'Of course she will,' Jeremy said, trying to sound more positive than he felt. Mrs Masters had barely shown any interest even when the pregnancy had gone so horribly wrong. She had also made it perfectly clear she didn't want to know until Alice had her life sorted. Privately Jeremy would have liked to have indulged in a few choice words with her but he knew it wasn't his place—yet. He hesitated for a moment, not wanting to tell Alice while she was in this mood that he really could only stay for five minutes. 'Alice, I have to get back to work, I'm on call tonight and there's an urgent lap choly scheduled this evening...'

'I'll be fine,' she said, trying to force a smile.

'What time are you being discharged?'

Alice forced her mind to concentrate 'Eleven a.m. Look, we can get a taxi. I know you'll be busy...'

But Jeremy was having none of it. 'I'll be here by eleven.' He leant over to give her a soft kiss goodnight but at the last moment she turned her face so his lips only grazed her cheek. 'I love you Alice,' he said almost pleadingly.

But Alice couldn't answer, and as he reluctantly left she

gave way to the tears that had been threatening all day. How could he love her like this? How could anyone love her when her own mother didn't even want to know? Glancing over at the crib, she watched Maisy sleeping on, oblivious to her mother's tears. She couldn't provide her own child with a father, couldn't finish her internship. Alice looked over at the bottle of formula in the jug on her locker. She couldn't even provide her own baby with breast milk.

'Only me.'

'Linda!' Alice blew her nose noisily on a handkerchief.

'I know it's after hours but the sister said you were still awake.'

'You just missed Jeremy,' Alice said quickly, searching for something to say to her surprise visitor. 'He had to rush back to do an urgent lap choly.'

Linda's forehead furrowed. 'Really? First I've heard about it.' Seeing the look of confusion flicker over Alice's face, she gave her a quick smile. 'But then what would I know?'

'But you're on call, aren't you?'

Linda shook her head. 'Not tonight—at least I certainly hope not,' she tried to joke, then, catching site of the crib, she swept over. 'Oh, Alice, she's beautiful. Josh said she was divine. Maisy, isn't it? Don't you just love those old-fashioned names?'

Alice couldn't help but be taken back by Linda's maternal tones but she forced a smile. After all, Linda was making an effort.

'So you're not on call?' Alice asked again, wondering if she'd misheard Jeremy.

'No, it's Mr Taylor's team tonight.' Linda gave her a questioning look. 'Why? Isn't work the last thing you should be worrying about with this little baby to look after?'

Alice gave a wry laugh without bothering to answer.

With Maisy to look after, work was one thing she definitely had to worry about. Almost on cue Maisy stirred in her crib and Linda wasted no time in asking if she might hold her.

'Sure,' Alice replied, trying desperately to ignore the knot of tension in her stomach. But Linda, it would appear, had eyes only for the baby. Swooping little Maisy up, she rocked her gently and Alice started to relax.

'She's beautiful, Alice, absolutely gorgeous. You must be so proud. I must admit, I do so admire you going it alone.' She glanced almost shyly over to where Alice lay. 'A dear friend of mine had a little boy a couple of years ago. I have no end of admiration for how she's coped. Mind you, she's had it tough.'

'In what way?' Alice asked, more to make conversation than out of interest. She had problems enough of her own without hearing about one of Linda's friends.

'Oh, you know, her boyfriend didn't want to know. Then suddenly when the baby was eighteen months old he found himself a nice wife, and after a year of trying with no babies coming he decided to file for custody.'

Seeing Alice's alarmed face, Linda seemed to realise the distress she had caused and begged to reassure her. 'But it's nothing like that for you. I'm sorry, Alice, I shouldn't have brought it up. Marianne—my friend—as much as I love her and everything, well, suffice it to say it wasn't straightforward like you. She'd had other boyfriends before, during and after the pregnancy, hardly the stuff to make you sound favourable in front of the family law court when you're up against the picture of domesticity—her ex-boyfriend and his charming stay-at-home wife. Still, it's not as if anything like that could happen to you—we all know how upset you were when it ended with your boyfriend. If push came to shove I'm sure the courts would come down in your favour. After all, you're the child's mother and a doctor, too. A good job must surely count for something.'

Alice somehow managed a polite murmur, but as Linda turned her attentions back to Maisy Alice felt the cold claws of panic clutching at her heart. Surely Marcus couldn't change his mind—surely not! But what if he did? What chance would an unemployed mother, living in a bed-sit, have against an affluent dentist and his kindergarten teacher wife? And as for Jeremy, if anyone wanted to fight dirty there was plenty room for mud-slinging there! Goodness, she hadn't even waited until the baby was born before jumping into bed with the biggest rake in hospital history.

Her first instinct was to grab Maisy back from Linda, to clutch her babe to her bosom and hold her, but Alice restrained herself, desperately trying to focus on the conversation. She was overreacting. Maisy was hers—surely there was no argument there?

'What happened in the end?'

'Sorry?' Linda gave her a bemused look.

'To your friend with the baby—what happened in the end?'

'Oh, it's still going on. The poor child spends half its time with each parent. Can't do it much good. Marianne is just about at her wits' end. I try to be as supportive as I can, but there's really not much I can do except listen, I guess, and try not to say "I told you so". Honestly, Alice, I'm only saying this because there's no chance of you meeting her, but I really have to bite my tongue sometimes. Marianne just carried on as if she was young, free and single. I know she's my friend and I know I don't speak from experience, but surely when you make the decision to have a baby sometimes you have to take the tough road. And if that means saying no to a hot date and staying home, well, surely that's what you have to do. The baby *has* to come first. But, then, I'm preaching to the converted. I know you'd think the same.' She gazed down at the now sleeping baby, her hard face softening somewhat. 'Wouldn't she, sweetie?' Linda crooned. 'Your mummy only wants what's best for you.'

Alice was saved from any further details by the round, smiling face of the paediatrician peering round the door. 'Sorry I took so long to get here,' Mary Healesville needlessly apologised as she came in. 'I got waylaid upstairs. I was just hoping to check Maisy over before I sign her discharge papers. I thought it would be nice to have a chat, see if you've got any questions before you take her home.'

Linda handed Maisy back to Alice. 'I'll be off, then. It was lovely seeing you, Alice.' She smiled at the paediatrician. 'It's Mary Blake, isn't it? You were a couple of years below me at medical school.'

'That's right. I thought you looked familiar.' Mary shook Linda's hand. 'Actually, it's Healesville now, I got married last year. How about you?'

'Oh, still McFarlane,' Linda replied with a slight edge to her voice. 'Work doesn't leave me much time for anything else. I'm working for Jeremy Foster now, not that you'd know it—he's been sick most of the time I've been on his team.'

'Oh, yes, he's the one who had the big accident. It must be good to have him back.' Mary turned to Alice, obviously concluding the conversation, but Linda still lingered.

'Well, the young girls seem to think so, it doesn't matter how nicely you try to warn them. They still think they'll be the one that will change him and bring him to heel. That man leaves a trail of broken hearts everywhere. When will these girls realise that a man will say anything and I mean *anything*, to get a girl into bed, and it always ends in tears?'

'Oh, well, you live and learn,' Mary said pleasantly, rolling her eyes for Alice's benefit. 'It was nice catching up with you, Linda, but I'll have to ask you to excuse us now. I really need to get on.'

Thankfully Linda took her cue this time and left quietly. Only when the door was safely closed did Mary speak. 'Is she a friend of yours?'

'Not really,' Alice replied diplomatically. 'A colleague.'

Mary gave a knowing smile. 'That'd be right, you can choose your friends.'

'I take it she wasn't the most popular girl at medical school?'

'I'll say, and from what I've heard not much has changed. Now, on to far more pleasant matters—how's this gorgeous girl of yours doing? I see she's back over her birth weight.'

'No thanks to me.'

Mary sat down on the bed. 'The breastfeeding's still not going well, then?'

Alice's eyes brimmed and she shook her head, biting on her lip to stop the tears.

'Alice, I know she's not tiny, like some of the premmies on special care, but she was still very small. With all the publicity you'd be forgiven for thinking that just under two kilos is a normal birth weight. Well, let me tell you it's not. These little ones take for ever to feed, they get easily exhausted from sucking and just when the first feed's over it's almost time to do battle for the next. It isn't any wonder breastfeeding doesn't always go well.'

'But surely it's important, particularly with her being small, that I keep on trying. The midwives said—'

'Alice, listen to me, please.'

Alice stopped talking and stared at Maisy lying innocently in her arms.

'Enjoy her, love her. That's what's most important. Don't get too bogged down in trying to do everything perfectly. They're pretty tough, these little ones. You're her mother and your best is more than good enough. Don't let anyone tell you otherwise.'

And when it was only Maisy and Alice left, and she'd struggled through yet another lengthy feed and Maisy had fallen into a rather more exhausted than contented sleep, Alice, hating herself for her lack of trust, finally picked up the telephone.

'Melbourne City Hospital. Can I help you?'

'It's Dr Masters here. I was wondering if you could tell me which surgical team is on call tonight.'

'One moment, please, Dr Masters.' The wait was agony but finally the switchboard operator with a rustle of papers came back on the line and Alice held her breath as she awaited the information. 'Mr Taylor's the on-call surgeon tonight—can I page him for you?'

'No, that won't be necessary. Thank you.'

With a shaking hand she replaced the receiver and picked up the electric breast-pump from her bedside locker. Attaching the beastly shield to her breast, Alice flicked on the switch and lay there staring at Maisy as the rhythmic pumping of the machine tried to cajole the milk from her hopelessly unyielding breasts. If only, Alice thought ruefully as she labelled the paltry offering and wandered down to the fridge to store it, she was as successful at expressing as she was at crying. The tears she had shed would surely have stocked the fridge for a week.

That night was the worst yet. Perhaps sensing her mother's tension, Maisy was increasingly fretful, and sitting rocking her newborn, as the other babies seemed to slumber endlessly Alice had plenty of time to think.

She loved Jeremy, that was a given. Loved the way he made her feel, the way his haughty, superior face softened when he spoke to her. Loved the way he touched her, moved her, engulfed her senses. And she loved him for outwitting the odds and making it through. Even though he had a past she loved the man it had made him—knowledgeable, aware, even sensitive, and a wonderful lover. But sometimes love itself just wasn't enough. Now, after the months of waiting, a new person had come into her life. A little lady had exploded into Alice's universe and she needed a mother, and not any old mother. The best mother in the world.

A year ago, or even a couple of weeks ago, Alice would have been prepared to hedge her bets, to ride out the storm and see where her relationship with Jeremy was leading. But now... Now she was a mother, the only parent of a beautiful daughter. What right did she have to jeopardise Maisy's security by chasing a dream?

And Jeremy was a dream, Alice acknowledged with an involuntary sigh. How could she ever hold him? What chance did she have of holding the man dreams were made of, with a new baby, no job and strapped to a breast-pump for heaven knew how long? What competition was she against the Olivias and Carries of the world? What sort of life was she going to lead if she doubted his every move, had to ring to check where he was, if he really was on call? And when it all soured, as it surely would, who would suffer most? Maisy.

'Can I get you a warm drink?' Alice jumped slightly as the midwife spoke. 'Sorry, I didn't mean to startle you, it's these rubber soles.'

'No, I'm fine, thanks. I think she's finally gone off.' Easing herself out of the rocking chair, she gently laid Maisy into her crib then kissed the softest of cheeks. 'Goodnight, darling,' Alice whispered, pulling the bunny rug around Maisy's tiny shoulders. It was Maisy that mattered and, much as it galled her to agree with Linda, for once Alice acknowledged maybe she was right. It was time to take the tough road, to focus on her baby instead of herself. Her mind made up, Alice made her way wearily back to bed. Slipping between the sheets, she felt a spasm of fear. Tomorrow she would leave the safety of the hospital. There would be no midwives, no doctors and, worst of all, no Jeremy.

Now all she had to do was tell him.

Alice deliberated long and hard as to how she was going to tell Jeremy. Her first instinct had been to discharge herself early and maybe explain later, but she knew this was unfair, and also there was some security in telling Jeremy in the hospital. There was surely less chance of there being a scene in the middle of the maternity ward. But as the clock edged past eleven-fifteen Alice wondered if she had been worrying about Jeremy's reaction unnecessarily. Perhaps he had decided already that Alice and Maisy were simply too much to take on.

Finally he arrived. 'Sorry I'm late.' He placed a breathless kiss on her cheek. 'Oh, doesn't she look beautiful?'

Maisy did look beautiful, dressed for the first time in 'real' clothes—a cherry-red one-piece with a matching red beret swamped her tiny frame. It was one of the many outfits Jeremy had bought her.

'Are you all ready for the off?'

Alice swallowed hard. 'What's this?' she asked, prolonging the agony as she pointed to a padded velour baby car seat, which looked impossibly new and ludicrously expensive. 'I was going to hire a capsule from the hospital.'

'Well, then, I've saved you a job,' he said lightly, scooping up Maisy and carefully strapping her into the seat. 'I bought the nurses a huge cheesecake. I thought you might like to give it to them for their morning tea. Is there anything else you need to do?'

It would seem Jeremy had planned for everything—everything except the words that faltered from Alice's lips.

'You didn't have to do all that.'

'I know.' He grinned. 'I wanted to.'

'You might wish you hadn't after you hear what I've got to say.' She watched his face slip as she broke the news. 'I'm sorry if I've misled you Jeremy, but I can't go on seeing you.'

'What do you mean?'

Alice swallowed a huge lump. 'Just that. I've been doing a lot of thinking. You know—about me and Maisy and how it has to be. And it can't be with you. I have to do this alone.'

Jeremy shook his head fiercely. 'No, you don't. Alice, you *don't*. Whatever the problem is, we can sort it out. I love you, Alice, don't shut me out now.'

But Alice was adamant. 'It's not going to work. It's better this way.'

'Better? Better! Better for who?'

'For all of us,' she tried to reason. 'You could have anyone, it's just your confidence is low at the moment. Sooner or later you'll get back on your feet and realise the mistake you've made, and then you'll hurt us. Not deliberately, maybe, but the day will come.'

'No,' Jeremy denied. 'No, it won't. I know that you and Maisy are what I want.'

'For now. But she's not your baby, Jeremy. One day down the track you're going to realise what you've taken on and wonder what the hell you've done. You'll look at Maisy and see she's not yours.'

She had known it would be difficult, but seeing tears in his eyes, his beautiful strong face crumpled and destroyed, Alice felt like the biggest bitch in the world.

'How can you say that?' he demanded. 'How can you say that when every time I look in her eyes I only see you. I promised Maisy that first night, when you were sleeping and I held her, I promised her I would always be there for her, always do my best for her.'

For a second she wavered. Maybe she was wrong. Maybe

she could be the one to hold him. But as Maisy let out a tiny wail she fought back her doubts. She had to stay strong.

'It wasn't your place to be making those sorts of promises. I'm sorry, Jeremy.'

'Everything all right?' Bridgette's concerned face appeared at the door.

'Fine,' Alice said, trying to compose herself. 'I was just about to ring for a taxi.

But Jeremy stood firm. 'She's not going home from a hospital in a taxi.' He picked up the handle of the car seat. 'At least let me do this for her.'

And so Bridgette came down with them to the car park. The bright sun seemed alien to Alice after so long indoors. Her legs felt unsteady and unused to the distance. Jeremy's car didn't look quite so sophisticated with a huge bolt and baby-seat holder strapped in place.

'All fitted correctly.' Bridgette tried to lighten the mood. 'You are good. More often than not, the bolt's still in the wrapper and I'm asked to install it. I should start charging.'

Jeremy gave a thin smile. 'That was nearly me. I spent the morning fiddling in the garage, then finally had to admit defeat and rush back to the shop to beg them to help. That's why I was late,' he added.

The journey home was a nightmare. Neither tried to make small talk—the only saving grace was that Maisy slept. Any attempt at independence for Alice was further thwarted when they arrived at her flat. She carried Maisy in as Jeremy followed with her endless bags. Opening the door, she thought her heart would burst as she held back the tears. No wonder he had been late. Everywhere she looked there were pink balloons and streamers, a huge banner proclaiming WELCOME HOME, a bottle of champagne chilling in the sink, surrounded by ice. A huge basket of goodies was awaiting her inspection. She stood there quite still, surveying his work, unable to speak as she heard him come up the hallway and enter the flat.

'That's everything. I'll be off, then. I expect you want to be alone now.'

Bending down, she started to unclasp Maisy. 'You'd better take this.'

'Keep it,' he said grimly.

'What would I need a car seat for, Jeremy? I haven't even got a car.'

'You still have to get taxis. You can use it with car seat belts—it doesn't need the bolt.' And then Jeremy fired the parting shot. 'Anyway, what would I need it for, Alice? Now that I don't have you.'

CHAPTER EIGHT

SOMEHOW Alice stumbled through the next few weeks. Her tiny flat only seemed to get smaller as Maisy's ever-increasing accoutrements took over. The sink seemed to be forever flowing with mountains of used bottles waiting to be sterilised. Her laundry basket was growing like a weed in compost and was threatening to invade the couch. The already cramped bathroom was now filled with baby baths and endless creams and ointments, all proclaiming to be the one that would get rid of Maisy's infantile eczema. No matter how many times she tidied and vacuumed and ironed it was time to start again. Even a hasty morning shower and a quick drag of the comb seemed decadent when Maisy was wailing to be fed. It seemed like light years since she had last plucked her eyebrows—not that Maisy cared, Alice consoled herself.

Despite the dark gloom that seemed to have descended indelibly on her life, her one shining light through it all was Maisy, and every day Alice marvelled at the miracle she had been blessed with.

Wearily climbing the stairs to the flat one day, weighed down with Maisy and a pile of freshly laundered Babygros, her mood lifted somewhat at the sight of Josh, standing grinning at her door.

'Dianne's holding a coffee morning for her fellow post-natal depressees. Not wanting to be left out, I swiped a coffee cake and thought I'd hold my own.'

'You're not wrong there.' Josh had been marvellous since she'd come home, popping in and out, not remotely fazed by Alice's tears and self-doubt.

'You'd be banned in a moment if you tried to get in,' he joked as he followed her in. 'They're all insisting on the merits of breastfeeding to get one's pre-pregnancy figure back, and here's you not a gram over fifty kilos with little Maisy happily on the bottle.'

'Don't go there, Josh,' she warned with a half-smile; her abandoned breastfeeding still irking.

'So, how are things?' he asked after making the coffee and dishing up two huge slices of cake.

Alice shrugged. 'Not the best. I've just spent the most humiliating morning of my life trying to explain to a clerk at the unemployment centre how a doctor can only work as a doctor once she's completed her internship. And how, just because the baby's father is a fully qualified dentist, that doesn't stop him being the biggest—'

'Alice,' Josh chided, 'that's not the sweet, smiling girl I used to know.'

'I'm sorry.' Alice blushed. 'I'm sure you don't need to hear my tales of woe. How are things with you?'

Josh fiddled with the fork, pushing his cake around the plate. 'Like a minefield,' he admitted. 'We spend most of the time trying to reassure each other that Eamon is every bit as bright as Declan, and then Declan goes and coos and gurgles or tries to roll over while poor little Eamon lies there, staring at the ceiling, and either Dianne or I crack.'

Alice put her plate down and moved along the sofa, reaching out for her friend. 'It's early days yet, Josh. He's been through so much, it's just too soon to try and compare.'

'I know, I know, but sometimes I get so scared for him.'

Glancing over at Maisy, lying on a rug, her little legs almost chunky now cycling the air in jerky movements, Alice knew then that she was the lucky one. For all the complications, for all the risks, she had a healthy baby. It made her hellish morning at the unemployment centre look like a trip to the circus.

'I'm sorry, Josh. Here's me banging on about my problems when you've got more than enough of your own.'

Josh managed an engaging grin. 'But yours are so much more refreshing. While I've got you on a guilt trip, tell me, Dr Masters, exactly what did happen between you and the dashing Mr Foster?'

Mumbling, Alice retrieved her plate and took a hefty bite of her coffee cake. 'I guess my bump didn't quite act as the crucifix you so eloquently predicted.'

'So what went wrong?' Josh probed.

Alice stared at the cake for an age, then her eyes looked over to where Maisy lay. 'I grew up.' Her voice was almost a whisper and Josh had to strain to catch what she was saying. 'Maisy needs security, and asking for that from Jeremy would be like asking for the moon.'

But Josh wasn't convinced. 'I like Jeremy, I always have. OK, I admit he's got the worst reputation imaginable, and that this time last year I'd have cracked up laughing at the thought of him changing nappies and burping a baby, but, Alice, Jeremy has changed.'

'So he tried to tell me.'

'Then why can't you believe him?'

She couldn't answer. In truth she didn't know herself where the rot had set in, where the doubts had started. But now as she sat there, scared, terrified of the future and as lonely as hell, it was an impossible dream to imagine Jeremy Foster could ever love her again.

'Alice, what went wrong?'

The cake seemed to have turned to sand. Swallowing hard, she turned her reddened eyes to Josh and for the first time that day looked at him. 'I really don't want to talk about it.'

'Fair enough,' Josh said wisely. 'But maybe you'll want

to talk about this. You know Mai Wing filled your position practically immediately?'

Alice nodded, trying and failing to appear interested as she started to fold her washing.

'Well, as usual Linda was bitching, and for once it actually made sense. Mai Wing started her internship three weeks early, which means she's going to finish three weeks early...'

Alice clutched the tiny Babygro to her chest. 'So the team will be short.'

'Got it in one. Now, in a month's time little Maisy will have had her jabs and be able to go to the crèche, which means that you, Dr Masters, will be more than able to step in and finish your internship.

'But what about the on calls?' Alice ventured, unable to believe it could really be that that simple.

'There wouldn't be that many, and if push came to shove I'm sure Dianne could manage one more.'

'Don't be ridiculous,' Alice retorted. 'She's got enough to deal with.'

'Well, I could chuck a couple of sickies and stay home to help. It would make your night a lot longer but, hell, Alice, it's only three weeks. Surely between us we can work it out.'

Suddenly there was a light at the end of the tunnel. It could work, it really could! She could complete her internship, start her GP rotation, get out of the bedsit and give Maisy the security she deserved. The only obstacle was Jeremy. Would he agree? And, more to the point, even if he did there was the fact that she would have to see him again, to work alongside him. Looking at Maisy mindlessly pedalling the air, the figures on her mobile making her go cross-eyed as she attempted to focus, Alice felt her heart-rate quicken. For that little girl she could get through anything.

'So do you want me to talk to Jeremy?'

Her eyes sparkling, her cheeks flushed, Alice threw down the laundry and made her way over to Josh. 'Yes.' She nodded breathlessly, 'Yes, please.'

The hows and whys, the practicalities of going back to work so soon, were only starting to surface when her door-bell rang later. Checking that the noise hadn't disturbed Maisy, Alice pulled open the door, her smile rapidly disappearing as she saw Jeremy standing there.

'J-Jeremy,' she stammered.

He didn't answer for a moment, his eyes, like the first time they had met, flicking over her body, taking in the huge changes. It was then she realised it was the first time he had seen her slim. But even that did nothing to bolster her confidence as she was achingly aware she must look a fright. She had wanted to look so cool and sophisticated the next time they met.

'I have a proposition for you.' His voice was stilted, wooden even, but what did she expect? Pulling the door fully open, she gestured for him to come through. Josh must have spoken to him straight away. Safe in the knowledge that she knew what he was about to say, Alice gestured to the sofa, hesitantly sitting down herself, desperate yet totally unable to meet his eyes.

'As you know, we found a replacement for you straight away when you were taken ill.' His sharp tones ruled out the need for small talk as he headed straight to business. 'Well, the upshot is it would have left us short for three weeks at the end of the rotation.'

Alice didn't answer, not wanting to appear too keen. But her solemn face slipped into one of despair as Jeremy continued.

'Mai Wing—your replacement—has just had some bad news from overseas. Obviously she has no choice but to fly home. Now, I had initially been intending to offer you the position at the end of Mai Wing's rotation, but now that isn't an option.'

Alice felt the slimy walls of panic closing in again. Just when there had seemed some hope, a way out of the mess she was in, it had been snatched back. She hardly listened as Jeremy went on. 'However, I've told Mai Wing to take a full three weeks—that will bring us into line with the rest of the rotations when she's finished. Which leaves us short for now. I've spoken with Mr Felix and, given the circumstances and our heavy workload, he's agreed that we can offer you the chance to complete your internship. You can start on Monday—three weeks from now you could be fully qualified and off to the country. How about it?'

'Monday?' she gasped. 'I can't. I'm not making excuses, Jeremy, it just isn't possible. Maisy hasn't had her inoculations yet so no crèche will take her.' She thought of Josh's kind offer but knew she couldn't land this on him and Dianne—they had more than enough troubles of her own. Her mind flashed to her mother. 'I could try Mum…' she said doubtfully, knowing deep down it would be useless.

'There's no need to do that,' Jeremy said crisply. 'I knew before I offered you the position the obstacles you'd be up against, and I've got something to run by you. You may or may not recall I told you my mother first came to us as a nanny. Well, she's a fully qualified mothercraft nurse. She's kept her registration up and still does casual shifts at the local crèche now and then. She's always eager for any excuse to come down and stay with me and fuss. I've spoken to her and she's more than happy to look after Maisy.'

'I could never afford—'

'For God's sake, Alice, not everything comes down to money,' he snapped.

'It does when you're broke,' she retorted, flushing at revealing her plight.

'As if I'd offer if we were going to charge you. The only down side is that there's no way my mother would stay here.' He seemed almost to sneer as he looked around her flat. 'Which would mean you'd have to move into my place for the duration.'

'So my flat's not good enough?' Why she was being argumentative she didn't know, but Alice couldn't stop herself.

'Frankly, no.' Hell, he could be such a snob sometimes, and yet seeing his hostile face, knowing the pain she had caused and, more importantly, all they had been through together, she understood his contempt. Coming here today would have been hard.

'Why are you doing this for me?' she asked, genuinely bewildered that he would go to all this effort for her, but Jeremy wasted no time in shattering any illusions she might have had.

'Let's get one thing straight.' His eyes bored into her, cold and distant. She could almost taste the bitterness in his words as he spat out his speech. 'I'm not doing any of this for you. I'm doing it for Maisy. You may have chosen to disregard what I said about turning over a new leaf, but let me tell you this. I made a promise to Maisy and I fully intend to keep it. She deserves better than this.' He gestured to the untidy room, the overflowing ironing basket, the small electric fan battling fruitlessly against the oppressive afternoon heat.

'And you've got a chance now to give it to her. I don't expect you to make up your mind straight away, but I shall need to know by tomorrow morning. Personnel will need to be informed and obviously my mother will need to make some arrangements.' He put down a manila envelope on the coffee-table beside the remains of the coffee cake.

'These are my mother's certificates of registration. I know you won't want to take my word.' Picking up his car keys, he seemed to freeze on the spot as Maisy let out an indignant wail.

Alice walked over to the crib. Picking up her baby, she rocked her quietly against her, smelling the fragrance of baby powder and milk.

'She's grown,' Jeremy said softly. Looking up, Alice saw all the contempt had gone from his eyes, his features mellowing as he gazed on her daughter.

Alice took a deep breath. Jeremy was right, Maisy did deserve more. 'I don't need time to think about it. I'd like to start work on Monday.' She picked up the envelope and handed it to Jeremy. 'And of course I don't need to check the details; it's a very kind offer. Thank you.'

'Fine. I'll pick you up on Saturday morning. Can you be ready by ten?'

'Saturday? But…'

His face hardened again as his eyes flicked back from Maisy to Alice. 'As my mother is going to be looking after Maisy from seven-thirty on Monday morning it might be prudent for them to have some time together. Don't make the mistake of thinking you're going to be in for an easy ride over the next three weeks, Alice. You're not pregnant now.'

That was unfair. She had never asked for favours because of her condition, but, achingly aware of the pain she had caused him, she let it go. For a moment she'd thought Jeremy was softening.

'It will do you good to get back to work,' he said more kindly as he opened the door, but her illusion was soon shattered. 'Who knows? It might even give you a reason to wash your hair.'

*   *   *

She felt like a refugee as Jeremy loaded her bags and cases into his boot.

'That the lot?'

'I think so. I can always come back for anything I've forgotten.'

Checking for the third time that Maisy was correctly secured, she finally made her way around to the front seat and clipped on her belt. Aware of Jeremy's eyes on her, she felt a blush starting to creep over her face. 'What?' she asked rudely.

'Nothing. I was just thinking your hair looked nice.'

Alice shrugged dismissively. 'I just had a trim.' Which was a downright lie if ever she'd told one. Jeremy's comment had hit home and she had finally thrown caution to the wind and taken her credit card up to its limit, having a few low-lights and a deep conditioning treatment, as well as her legs waxed and her eyebrows plucked. Feeling somewhat more secure of her ability to provide now her work problem was sorted, she was more than aware she had let herself go somewhat. Alice wanted to look smart for her colleagues and patients—and Jeremy, she thought reluctantly before pushing the thought firmly away. That door was most definitely closed. She had made her choice and now she had to stick with it.

Any concerns she had about leaving Maisy with a stranger were laid to rest almost as soon the door to Jeremy's apartment flew open and Mavis Foster engulfed Alice and Maisy in a huge scented hug.

'You're here at last. Welcome, welcome. Don't just stand there. Come on through.'

'I'm sure Alice would if you gave her a chance,' Jeremy said dryly, but his eyes were smiling as he spoke to his mother.

'You poor thing. You must be terrified about going back

to work, but you mustn't fret. Work will be a breeze after the last few weeks.'

'Nice to hear you take my career so seriously,' Jeremy commented as he staggered in with the baby bath filled with bags. 'That's the last of it. I'll load up my stuff and be off, then. I'll see you at work on Monday, Alice.'

'Monday? But where are you going?'

'Off to Sorrento for the weekend. I thought you might find it easier to settle in without me interfering.'

Jeremy smiled as he spoke but his eyes were cold. He was obviously making an effort to appear friendly in front of his mother. Although he was probably right, and she should have felt relief at the reprieve, Alice could only feel disappointment.

'Right, Mum, I'll see you Monday night.' Alice was touched at the way he hugged and kissed Mavis goodbye.

'Right you are, darling. I'll have your favourite dinner waiting—steak and chips, just as you like them.'

Jeremy rolled his eyes and turned to Alice. 'My mother hasn't yet heard of oven chips, she still fries them in lard, and she won't believe me when I tell her that eggs and bacon no longer qualify as a healthy start to the day.'

'Rubbish,' Mavis retorted. 'A man needs a good breakfast.' She gave him a final kiss and insisted on standing at the door, waving, till the lift door closed. 'Right, Alice, before this baby of yours wakes up, how about we have a nice cup of tea and some cake and you can tell me all about her little ways?'

That night, groaning as she climbed into bed, Alice found she was actually smiling into the darkness. Full, fit to burst from a huge roast dinner and the stodgiest treacle pudding imaginable, she'd had to plead for mercy when Mavis had appeared at ten p.m. with a tray of toasted cheese for 'supper'. Who would have thought, Alice mused, that Jeremy, the coolest of cool men, would have a mother literally dripping with maternal instinct. You could just imagine her whipping out a handkerchief to wipe away a smudge from his cheeks at his graduation ceremony. More importantly, Mavis had been an absolute marvel with Maisy. Not interfering or superior, she had listened carefully as Alice had taken her through her baby's routine—not that she really had one; it was more hit and miss at the moment.

Over the weekend Alice felt her confidence grow, not only with leaving Maisy but more amazingly her own ability as a mother. Mavis seemed to instil in her a quiet confidence that as Maisy's mother she really did know best. If only her mother could have shown half as much interest, life could have been so much easier.

In fact, by Monday, as she stepped off the tram and headed into the hospital, Alice's only concerns were for the day ahead. She knew beyond doubt that Maisy was in the best possible hands.

'Welcome back, stranger.' Josh let out a low whistle. 'My goodness, you do look the part. What happened to the girl I left on Thursday?'

'Two hours in the hairdresser's and a ton of foundation. I'm so nervous, Josh. I feel as if I've forgotten everything.'

Josh gave her a friendly pat on the arm. 'Don't worry, one look at Linda and it will all come flooding back with painful familiarity. She's really in a strop this morning—her hormone tablets must have run out.'

Josh was right. Two hours into the day Alice felt as if she'd never been away. The ward round had been mercifully quick, with mostly discharges which meant heaps of empty beds and therefore heaps of admissions, but as they weren't the team on call that day hopefully she was in a for a fairly smooth first day back.

Famous last words. 'Alice, could I borrow you a moment?'

Alice looked up from the IV charts she was writing, glad of the diversion. She was desperate to ring Mavis and check on little Maisy but she had already rung once this morning. 'Sure, Fi, what's the problem?'

'It's Mrs Dalton.'

Alice nodded. Mrs Dalton had been Alice's last patient before she had gone off sick. During that time she had been discharged, only to return last week with the same problem. However, this time her ulcer was far worse and her circulation was deteriorating markedly. She was booked for an angiogram that morning to assess the severity of the blockage, and it was looking as if bypass surgery was becoming the only option.

'Her foot seemed fine on the ward round—well, no worse anyway. But she just buzzed and is saying it's agony. It feels pretty cold. I think you'd better take a look.'

Alice made her way straight over and as Fi pulled the curtains Alice slipped the bedsock off the offending foot.

'It's very painful, is it, Mrs Dalton?'

'Yes, dear. I'm sorry to make such a fuss; I know you're all busy.'

Alice looked up from the foot to her patient. 'Let's have none of that. Now, when did the pain start?'

'Just after Mr Foster left. I tried to ignore it…'

Alice knew from her previous conversations with Mrs Dalton that for her to be this distressed meant that she was in severe pain. Mrs Dalton had put up with more than enough in her life without complaint. The foot was definitely cold, not just cool, and there was some mottling around the toes and on the dorsal surface. Gently she tried to palpate the pedal pulse but after a few moments of effort and quiet concentration she took her fingers away. 'Did you have any luck, Fi?'

'No.'

Fi handed her the Doppler, and Alice squeezed some gel

onto the cold foot. Gently placing the probe, she tried to find a pulse. The speaker made some whooshing noises as Alice slowly and patiently moved it around, but despite all her efforts there was definitely no pulse to be heard.

'Shall I page Jeremy for you?'

Alice chewed her lip. 'Better not. Can you try Linda first?'

The attempt at friendliness on Linda's part obviously only extended to out of hours. Her sour voice on the end of the phone was back to its usual condescending tones and when she marched into the ward she didn't even bother to address Alice, instead directing all her questions at Fi.

'How long has it been like this?' she barked.

'Mrs Dalton said the pain started after the ward round.'

'But that was over an hour ago. Why was it left so long before calling someone? Were you waiting for it to turn blue?'

'I only just let the staff know,' Mrs Dalton said apologetically, and Alice choked back her own rage at Linda's unprofessional attitude.

'Should I page Mr Foster?' Fi ventured.

'He's already coming,' Linda barked. 'It was obvious to *me* this was an emergency.'

Which it was, of course, but, as Alice had done, Jeremy took his time examining the foot, carefully trying to palpate a pulse, listening with the Doppler and arranging a strong injection for pain while he waited for the ultrasound machine to arrive.

'It doesn't look too good, does it, Doctor—I mean Mister?'

Jeremy looked up from the ultrasound monitor. 'There's a blood clot blocking off the blood supply,' Jeremy informed her, his voice friendly but entirely professional. 'Now, we could start a heparin infusion, that would thin the blood and disperse the clot, but the down side is that may take too long. Realistically I think we ought to take you straight to Theatre and perform what we call an embolectomy. While we're there we'll also perform the bypass surgery to hopefully improve the circulation to your foot.'

'And if it doesn't work?'

Alice found herself staring at her own feet as she awaited Jeremy's answer.

'Well, I'm going to do everything I can to make sure that it does work but, yes, there is a chance, and a fair one, that it mightn't work.' He paused, allowing his words to sink in.

'You'd have to amputate?'

'Worst-case scenario, yes.' He waited a couple of moments as Mrs Dalton sobbed quietly into her handkerchief before he continued. 'Mrs Dalton, I don't like to speculate too much, and I don't like to raise false hope, but certainly that is really a last resort. My intention is to save your foot.'

For the next fifteen minutes Mrs Dalton's bedside was a hive of activity. The anaesthetist came in to do a pre-op assessment. Thankfully, as she had been due for an investigation later that morning, Mrs Dalton was already fasting, which made emergency surgery a lot safer as her stomach was empty, thus reducing the risk of aspiration. Fi, quietly efficient, performed an ECG without waiting to be asked, and by the time Mr Dalton had arrived, red in the face and dressed in the grubby jeans and an old T-shirt, Mrs Dalton was ready to be taken to Theatre.

'Fancy coming to the hospital in your gardening clothes,' Mrs Dalton chided, groggy from the analgesia. 'What will people think?'

'Never satisfied, these women, no matter what you do,' Mr Dalton tried to joke as his eyes filled with tears.

'I quite agree,' Jeremy quipped, and Alice was positive *that* little comment was aimed at her.

But there was none of that once they got to Theatre. The

only objective here was to save Mrs Dalton the trauma of losing her foot and Jeremy worked exhaustively, first evacuating a huge clot before the painstaking task of bypass surgery. Finally, when it was over, Alice could only again marvel at his skill. Mrs Dalton's foot, right down to the tips of her toes, was now a healthy pink.

'I want strict fifteen-minute vascular obs for the first two hours, then hourly for six hours and two-hourly overnight. Actually, make it hourly overnight.'

'The ward staff won't be too pleased,' Carrie warned.

'Do I look as if I care?' snapped Jeremy, peeling off his gloves and hurling them into the metal bin beside Mrs Dalton's gurney before stalking out of the recovery room.

Carrie raised a well-plucked eyebrow. 'Someone's unhappy in love. I wish I knew who she was—I'd like to buy her a drink. It's about time that bastard got his comeuppance.'

The venom in Carrie's voice was pure poison, and as she listened Alice felt the hackles on her neck rise. 'I'd like to remind you, Sister, that Mr Foster happens to be my boss and a consultant surgeon. If you can't show any respect for that fact then at least show it for your patient. Mrs Dalton may be unconscious but there can be no excuse for that kind of talk.'

'I'm sorry,' Carrie spluttered, the colour in her cheeks mounting. 'It won't happen again.'

'It had better not,' Alice warned. 'Let's leave it there, shall we?'

Making her way to the changing rooms, Alice realised she was shaking. Useless at confrontation, she normally avoided it. But hearing Jeremy so unfairly being jeered at, she had felt anger flame within her. Sitting herself down on the small wooden bench, she put her head into her hands. Who was she trying to kid? She loved him, she always had, she had never stopped. It was just so impossible. Even if she wanted to ignore his past, everywhere in this hospital there were constant reminders. Maybe it was for the best. Maybe that would serve to keep her strong and focussed and remember why she could never be with him again. Letting him go once had been agony, to do it again would be sheer hell.

CHAPTER NINE

IF THERE was some tension at work between them, it was almost bearable. Jeremy was aloof and distant, but the demands of their busy schedules and the vast difference in their status meant there was, more often than not, a reason to rush off if things got too close for comfort. But on the home front the tension was palpable. Jeremy did his utmost not to be there and, given the fact that Alice was a mere intern, it invariably meant her days were punishingly long. But there were the inevitable times when they met in the hallway on their way to the bathroom or had to make small talk over the vast three-course meals that Mavis insisted on cooking.

The one saving grace was Maisy. Her angelic presence always lightened the mood, and some evenings, when Alice was positive she would spontaneously combust if she had to sit there staring at the television with Jeremy achingly close as Mavis knitted quietly, she would jump with relief when Maisy let out her wakening cry.

He was wonderful with Maisy—there was no argument there. Though he was careful not to appear too keen when Alice was there, several times when she came home she hid a smile as she walked in to find Jeremy singing the latest pop songs to his devoted audience, or practising his lecture technique on the finer points of vascular surgery to his most affable student.

'Finally, a female who doesn't answer back.' He would shrug, blushing as Alice walked in. 'How could I resist?'

'Give her time, Jeremy. She'll learn.'

But there was too much left unsaid, too many questions

unanswered for there not to be some sort of confrontation, and three weeks was a long time when your heart was bleeding.

One night during the second week she was there Maisy was particularly fretful. Nothing Alice tried seemed to placate her. She tried more milk, boiled water, rocking her face down, as June Wicks, the maternal and child health nurse, had showed her, but nothing, it seemed, was going to silence her. Almost at her wits' end, Alice was tempted to knock on Mavis's door and ask for some welcome advice. But just when Alice had exhausted all possibilities and was about to beg the older woman's guidance Maisy, for no apparent reason, suddenly gave Alice the most delicious smile and drifted off into a deep sleep.

Wide awake now, Alice padded out to the kitchen with a pile of half-empty bottles and nappies. The sight of Jeremy sitting hunched at the kitchen table, nursing a glass, stopped her in her tracks. Suddenly she was back where it had all started, catching him unawares, glimpsing the Jeremy behind the cool façade. She was truly horrified by how he seemed to have aged—the blond stubble on his chin and the lines etched around his eyes. He didn't look up, but as she stood there, not knowing quite what to do, he spoke, his voice thick and husky.

'Is she all right?'

'She's just gone off. I'm sorry, Jeremy, I tried to keep her quiet. Are you in pain again?' she asked, knowing it was now none of her business but concerned just the same.

'Agony,' he replied. Jeremy took a sip of his drink and with a long sigh he placed the glass down on the table. 'Have you any idea the hell it is for me, listening to her crying?'

Alice was straight on the defensive. 'I said I tried to keep her quiet. Surely you must have known it might be like this sometimes with such a young baby. If it's too much we'll be out—'

He stopped her flood as he banged the glass down on the table. 'I meant listening to her crying and not being able to do anything, sitting here not being able to help because you've erected a damned ''do not enter'' sign around your heart. I'm sorry,' he said wearily, looking up at her stunned face. 'You don't need this. We're on call tomorrow. I'd better get to bed.'

'Can I fetch you a painkiller or anything?' she asked, not wanting to let him go like this.

A wry smile tugged at the edge of his lips. 'A painkiller wouldn't touch it.'

It was only when he had left the kitchen that Alice realised with a start that the agony he was in wasn't from his back. With a moan she realised it was she, Alice, that was causing his pain. The cool persona, the icy contempt, it was all an act—he really did love her.

Back in the sanctuary of her bedroom, gazing at Maisy asleep, one hand held high above her head as if she were doing some strange version on the Irish jig, Alice ached to go to him, to hold and comfort him—but what then? Her old fears were sniping at her heels again—Linda's painful predictions, Carrie's wrath, Olivia's pain. How could she risk Maisy and her security by throwing it away to chase a dream, delectable as it was? It took a massive effort to climb into bed, pull the sheets up tightly and will herself to sleep—anything rather than weaken now. She had come so achingly close to achieving her goals that it would be foolhardy to wreck it now.

After a night spent trying and failing not to think of Jeremy, the last thing Alice needed was the prospect of twenty-four hours on call. But Mavis, insisting she had slept like a log and hadn't heard a peep all night, fussed about seemingly oblivious to the tension, piling mountains of bacon and toast onto Alice's plate and refilling her cup with sweet, strong coffee.

'Come on. Jeremy,' she scolded gently as he appeared unshaven at the table. Obviously Jeremy wasn't relishing the prospect of being on call either. They studiously avoided each other's eyes as Mavis rabbited on. 'So if you get home before two tomorrow, fine, but if not I'll take Maisy to the child health nurse for her weigh-in. Is there anything you want me to ask for you?'

Alice had a list as long as her arm, but instead she shook her head. 'Just mention that she seems unsettled at night. I think she might even be teething, although it seems a bit soon.'

Mavis clucked happily. 'Some are born with teeth.'

'Anyway, I should be back in plenty of time to take her myself. I usually finish around midday after being on call.' She stood up, smoothing some crumbs from her smart navy skirt. 'I'd better be off.'

'But why not wait for Jeremy?' Mavis protested. 'He won't be too much longer, will you, pet?' she asked, turning to the newspaper now blocking Jeremy's face. 'It seems silly, you taking a bus or tram when Jeremy will be driving there anyway.'

'Perhaps she needs some fresh air,' Jeremy suggested curtly, not bothering to move the paper.

Planting a lingering kiss on Maisy's cheek as the baby gurgled happily in Mavis's arms, it was a positive relief to escape the unbearable tension of the apartment and step out into the warm morning sun. It was only just over a week until her internship was completed but it seemed interminable. Admitting to herself that she had never stopped loving Jeremy only made things harder, and the fact he obviously loved or at least thought he loved her made it downright impossible.

Even as she stepped on the tram, purchased her ticket

and made her way to her seat, her muddled mind never once left Jeremy. Resting her head against the cool window, she allowed her mind to wander. Suppose, and it was a big suppose, she did relent, did reveal the depth of her feeling to him and—almost more impossible—suppose he did forgive her, what then? Mavis wasn't going to be around for ever. Jeremy was hardly going to move to the country. Jeremy—with all his ego, all his immaculate, chauvinist, carefree ways—suddenly thrust into the role of a parent as she struggled to juggle work and child-raising—it could never last, and she was a fool to even hypothesise.

The wailing of a siren broke into her daydream. The tram halted at the lights, giving way as an ambulance sped past. As they waited, unmoving, through several light changes the air was filled with ever-increasing wails. Looking out, Alice saw a couple more ambulances tearing towards the hospital. Making her way to the head of the tram, she spoke to the conductor.

'What's the delay?'

'Police told us to sit tight, love. Apparently there's been a big accident. They're trying to keep the entrance clear.'

'Could you let me off?' Alice asked urgently. 'I'm a doctor, I'd better get there.'

'No worries, Doc.'

As the doors slid opened her mobile phone trilled loudly. Answering it as she ran, her heart came into her mouth as she heard the chilling message.

'Dr Masters, there's a major incident in progress. Can you please come directly to Accident and Emergency?' The switchboard operator's voice was cool and efficient but Alice could detect the tremor in it. She would have been given a list of all personnel to work through and would know exactly what to do after the endless rehearsals, but this was no mock set up. Alice knew for sure it was real.

'I'm on my way. I'll be two minutes,' she gasped as

ambulance after ambulance sped by. Something huge was going on.

The impeccable mechanism of the accident and emergency department had swung into action by the time Alice arrived, breathless, at the doors. Fay, the unit manager, donning a red hard hat to show she was in charge, was directing the traffic. 'Dr Masters, straight through to Resusc, please. Mr Donovan will direct you.'

'What happened?'

'Two buses versus a truck' came the grim reply. The casualty list would be huge.

What went up had to come down—it was a simple law of physics. On the up side, if there was to be a major incident, seven forty-five was probably the best time for it to happen. At that time the nurses were still in hand over, meaning there was double the staff. Most doctors were already there or, like Alice, on their way, while the night cover was still on site. The down side to the scenario was that if a truck lost control and collided with two buses, seven forty-five a.m. meant they would both be packed with commuters and school children.

Alice steeled herself as she entered the department in an attempt to prepare herself for what lay ahead. But despite lectures, videos and simulations of a major incident, nothing but nothing could have prepared her for the sight that greeted her. It was truly appalling. Bodies were everywhere as Samuel Donovan, the accident and emergency consultant, directed the staff while simultaneously working on patients.

Jeremy had obviously beaten her to it. He'd clearly not even had time to remove his jacket, and his immaculate grey suit was already splattered in blood as he worked on a lifeless body on the trolley in front of him. She watched as he shook his head and looked up at the clock, calling the time that this life had ended. For a second he caught her eye, and not for the first time Alice couldn't interpret the look that flashed over his face.

'Take this one into a cubicle, Alice,' Samuel ordered as the paramedics rushed a trolley in.

The young woman that met Alice's eyes as she looked down at the ambulance stretcher had a look of absolute terror on her face and Alice's heart went out to her for what she must have been through. Her face was as pale as the sheet that covered her, and Alice was certain that under normal circumstances she would have been placed straight into Resusc—but, then, there was nothing normal about today.

'This is Kim Earl, twenty-two years of age, passenger in bus number one. She was up the front end of the vehicle, which took most of the impact. When we got to her she was conscious, trapped by her left leg.'

The paramedic gave Alice a wide-eyed look and glanced down at the affected limb. Alice's gaze followed his. The leg was heavily splinted and covered in drapes, but Alice could see from the hideous angle at which the foot was lying and the colour of the toes the reason for the paramedic's concerned expression.

'She's also complaining of some abdominal pain, but her leg seems to be the main source of pain. She's had gas on the way with some relief.'

'Thanks very much.' Alice said when they had carefully moved Kim onto the hospital gurney. 'Are there many more to come?'

The lead paramedic gave a grim nod. 'Yep, we'd better get back to it. Oh, one thing we didn't tell you. Kim's due to get married on Saturday, aren't you, Kim?' He gave the terrified woman a friendly wink. 'They'll look after you now, Kim. Good luck. I'll come and see how you got on later.'

Alice was always impressed by the paramedics. The

scene they had just attended and were going back to would have been horrific, yet despite it all they had found the time to make the patient feel more than a number, to treat her as a young woman with a life and problems of her own, not just a nasty leg and abdo injury. It was a lesson Alice always tried to remember.

They had already established intravenous access, and as the nurses were all tied up Alice did a swift set of observations, trying to quell the mounting panic within her as she examined her patient. An accurate assessment was especially vital, given the fact that the senior staff were involved elsewhere. Kim's leg, the most obvious injury, was for the moment safely covered and secured, so there was no point concentrating on that if she had more dire injuries. Her neurological status was sound, Alice noted, with no apparent head injury apart from a few abrasions. Moving to her chest, Alice was satisfied her air intake was adequate with no breathing difficulty, though her respiration rate was high. Her abdomen, though, was distended and tender.

Alice felt a surge of anxiety. This young woman was seriously injured. Inserting another IV cannula, Alice took some baseline bloods and an urgent group and cross-match then attached a plasma expander drip. There were supplies of O-negative blood kept in the emergency department but these would already be sorely depleted. Samuel Donovan would have to ration that valuable commodity.

Alice rechecked Kim's blood pressure, which was markedly lower with her pulse-rate increasing, a sign of large blood loss. What would Jeremy do next? That was how she'd play it.

Peritoneal lavage. It was a relatively simple procedure which involved making a small incision into the abdominal cavity and allowing in a bag of warmed saline. If when the saline flowed back there was blood in it, it meant the patient needed to go to Theatre. Although a straightforward procedure, it was not one Alice had done before but, realising the seriousness of the situation, she prepared all the equipment that would be needed before rushing out.

'Mr Donovan?'

He made his way over swiftly. 'What have you got?'

'Twenty-two-year-old female with a serious leg injury, which I haven't looked at yet. It's her abdomen I'm more concerned about, though. I think she's bleeding out. I've set up for a peritoneal lavage.'

'Good.' He came straight to the gurney and, after briefly introducing himself, performed the procedure. 'She needs Theatre. OK, I'll get Jeremy. Fay…'

In a matter of ten minutes Kim was about to be taken up to Theatre. All planned ops had been cancelled to leave room for the urgent cases, and Kim couldn't wait.

'I'll see you on the ward.' Alice squeezed the young woman's hand. 'Mr Foster is going to operate.'

'What about my leg?'

It was Samuel Donovan who answered as the orthopods examined her leg.

'Kim, it's a very serious leg wound you have. We'll have a better idea in Theatre once you're anaesthetised. We'll do the X-rays up there.'

'It has to be right for Saturday.'

'She's getting married,' Alice said to the consultant.

Despite the chaos, despite the tragedies unfolding in all directions, Samuel took the time to explain to this beautiful young woman as he took her through the consent form that, although they would do everything to save her leg, it might not be possible.

'No!' The scream that emerged from Kim's lips was blood-curdling. 'I won't consent to that. You can't cut it off.'

Mr Khan, the orthopaedic consultant, came to the head of the gurney. 'Now, please, my dear, believe me when I say I'm going to do my utmost to save it, but it doesn't look good. I cannot and will not let you die from your leg wound. And that could be the reality. I'm not going to amputate unless I have no other choice.'

Kim looked pleadingly at Alice. 'Is that it? I'm going to lose my leg? Can't I get a second opinion? I've got private cover…'

For some reason, perhaps because she had been the first doctor present, perhaps because she was a woman or near her age, Kim needed Alice's opinion.

'Kim, when the doctors say they'll do everything, they mean it. You really need to go Theatre. I know how hard this must be.'

'No, you don't.'

Alice knew she was right. 'I'm sorry. I can only imagine—'

'Will I die?'

Alice squeezed her hand. 'We're not in the business of letting young women die. Our job is to do everything to save you, and that means you have to go to Theatre now.'

Kim's eyelids were starting to close and she struggled to open them.

'Ted, my fiancé…'

'I'll talk to him as soon as he gets here. He'll be waiting for you when you come out.'

Watching the pale, shaking hand as Kim signed the consent form, it took a superhuman effort for Alice to stay professional. Kim should be signing a marriage certificate in a few days, not a damned consent form that might render her an amputee.

Although the situation had intensified, with a seemingly never-ending stream of casualties still arriving at an alarming rate, the department seemed a lot more controlled. More staff were now present, many of them senior and able to make swift assessments and prioritise the patients. Up on the wards all patients who had arrived for planned surgery or were well enough to be discharged were being seen by doctors and sent home to free up beds for those that needed them. The overnight stay ward in the emergency department had become a makeshift mortuary.

Stunned, Alice still couldn't take in what she was a part of. The precarious line that held everyone inside a safe normality could change in an instant. Life that day had changed for all present.

'How's your stitching, Alice?' Fay grabbed her as she walked past. 'Do you mind making a start?'

And so she played her part. OK, so she wasn't up in Theatre saving a life or in the resuscitation room on the front line. But over the next five hours Alice knew that she was doing a good job. Painstakingly she picked out the never-ending lumps of shattered glass, applied local anaesthetic and cleaned aligned edges, doing her small bit to make sure the external scars people bore to remind them of this black day were as minimal as possible. Her soft voice was gentle, reassuring patients and their relatives. And sometimes when there was no need for words, when the patients just wanted to lie still and let her get on, Alice's mind drifted to Jeremy up in Theatre, doing his best to save a young woman's life. Jeremy, who had always done his best for her and later Maisy, too.

'Alice, when you finish this one, Kim Earl's parents and fiancé have arrived. I've done my best to talk to them but I was wondering if you might have a word. Samuel's not going to get there for ages and she's still in Theatre.'

'Sure, Fay,' Alice replied, placing a dressing over the hand she had just sutured. 'I'll come now.'

'A word of warning—the fiancé isn't taking it all too well.'

'Can you blame him?' Alice said sadly. 'It must be an awful shock.'

But Fay shook her head. 'His greatest concern is the fact she might lose her leg. Look, I'll let you judge for yourself. Just tread carefully.'

Bill and Sheila Earl looked every bit as devastated as any parents would, confronting the events that had been thrust upon them. Bill sat staring at the wall ahead, his heavily tattooed arm around his wife's shoulders. Sheila was gently rocking, not making a sound as tears coursed down her cheeks. A younger man, dressed in a trendy single-breasted charcoal-grey suit, his dark wavy hair cut closely to his head and slicked back with gel, introduced by Fay as Ted Caversham, paced relentlessly up and down the tiny room.

Alice pulled a chair up and sat down opposite the parents, and as gently as possible took them through her dealings with Kim.

'The sister said her injuries were serious.' Bill cleared his throat. 'How serious? She's not going to…?'

'She was bleeding internally, I'm not sure from where. Rather than wait for further investigations which would have taken up a lot of time, particularly due to the demand on equipment this morning, it was considered far safer to take her directly to Theatre. I'm sorry I can't be more specific, but I really don't know much more than that. However, what I can tell you is that she was taken to Theatre very quickly, and the surgeons that are operating are first class. She was conscious throughout. I spoke with her and she told me all about the wedding.'

A trembling smile wobbled on Sheila's lips, then as the realisation dawned again it vanished and she gave way to hysterical tears.

'But what about her leg?' Ted turned an angry stare on Alice. 'We've been told she might lose it.'

Alice swallowed. 'It does look a real possibility. Her leg was partially severed below the knee. I personally didn't see it but the orthopaedic consultant said that it was a very serious injury, though I must reiterate that everything will be done to save it.'

'Rubbish. They'll be rushing to get the next case in. I tell you now that if everything, and I mean everything, isn't done this hospital is going to have the biggest lawsuit—'

'Mr Caversham, I understand you're distressed—'

'You bet I'm distressed. You calmly walk in here and tell us that Kim's probably going to lose her leg—'

'The important thing,' Alice interjected, 'is that she gets out of Theatre. Once we know the extent of her injuries, the doctors can give more definitive answers to your questions. At the moment it's pure speculation.'

'If Kim loses her leg, she might as well die.' Alice fought to hold her tongue as Ted Caversham continued, 'You might think I sound harsh, but you don't know her. She's a model, for heaven's sake. She simply won't cope.'

Privately Alice rather thought it was Ted that wouldn't be able to cope with the loss. Standing up, she picked up her stethoscope from the coffee-table. 'As soon as we hear anything further, we'll let you know.' She wanted to stress that at the moment Kim's leg, although a tragedy in itself, was really the least of her problems, but bringing Ted down a peg or two could only exacerbate Bill's and Sheila's pain. 'I'm sorry I can't give you any more answers.'

Fay was waiting for her as she came out. 'A charmer, isn't he?'

'He's probably just upset. People react strangely.'

Fay gave her a knowing look. 'Yes, people react strangely, but I can't help but think he's more worried about his image than poor Kim. How all this is going to affect *him*.' Taking Alice's arm, she led her to the staff room. The canteen has sent down some refreshments.' With a final glance back towards the interview room Fay shook her head. 'Tell me, Alice, where have all the good guys gone?'

'Here's where you're hiding.'

Alice smiled as Josh entered, then flushed as she realised Jeremy was directly behind him. There was the answer to Fay's question. Jeremy looked terrible, his grim face set with tension. He had been operating without a break since eight-thirty that morning, and Alice couldn't help but wonder how he was coping with his back. Alice poured the two men coffee while Fay piled a couple of plates with sandwiches.

'I needed that.' Never had a cup of coffee and a cheese and Vegemite sandwich been more welcome.

Fay grinned. 'Me, too.'

Finally a sense of normality was emerging. Though A and E was still full, no case now was particularly urgent and a welcome break was most definitely in order. Glancing at her watch, Alice gave a yelp. 'Heavens, it's three o'clock! What time are you due to finish, Fay?'

'Seven hours ago' came the rueful reply.

'You were on last night? Oh, Fay, you must be exhausted.'

'Actually, no. I'm quite sure if I went to bed now I wouldn't be able to sleep. If you knew how much time I've spent in meetings and mock-ups, preparing for this day, hoping it would never happen but trying to be sure that if it did we'd be able to cope. I think we did well.'

'I don't think we could have done any better,' Josh agreed. 'Everyone was marvellous, pitching in. What was the final casualty count?'

'Fifty. We saw twenty-eight, the rest went on to the Women's and Children's or were flown to the trauma centre.'

'How many fatalities?'

Fay let out a long breath. 'Eighteen. Unbelievable, isn't

it? People like you or I just setting off to work or school. How's it going up in Theatre?'

Josh didn't answer until he had demolished a couple of sandwiches. 'Bloody awful—literally. There's a couple down here for Theatre still, aren't there, Fay?'

'Yep. When do you think you'll be able to do them?'

Jeremy stood up, speaking for the first time. 'Now. Theatre four was just finishing up.' He turned to Josh. 'You finish off your food. I'll go and see them then meet you in Theatre, say in half an hour.'

'How did Kim Earl do?' Alice called as he made to leave. She watched as his departing back stiffened. Turning only slightly, not meeting her eyes, he replied curtly, 'Perforated bowel, lacerated liver. She had to spend an age in Recovery but she should be transferred to the ward soon. Really she needs to be in Intensive Care, but those beds were snapped up long ago.'

'What about her leg?' Alice persisted. 'How did it go?'

'It didn't.' And without any further explanation he left the room. Fay raised an eyebrow.

'How's Jeremy? He went as white as a sheet when the call came in—it must have brought all the memories of his accident back.'

Josh didn't look convinced. 'He's seen enough trauma since he's been back, but maybe you're right. There's definitely something wrong.' He shot a look in Alice's direction. 'He's not exactly been sociable the past few weeks, but today he's far worse. There's something up—not that it's stopped him performing miracles I hasten to add. That guy's a brilliant surgeon; he's like a machine down there.'

'And Linda?' Fay asked, smiling as she anticipated a smart crack from Josh.

'Loving every moment. It's the most excitement she's had in years.' He gave a lewd grin before adding, 'Of any kind. First time I've seen her wearing lipstick. She's hoping to make it onto the news. Oh, well, back to it.'

The short interlude over. They all stood up, marginally refreshed, ready to do battle again.

Fi looked as immaculately in control as ever, her soft voice relaying instructions and answering queries as the ward struggled to cope with a mass of acutely injured patients as well as the usual workload.

'I'm not even going to ask if you've got anything for me, Fi. But thanks for holding off on the pager; I've been suturing down in A and E.'

'I knew you wouldn't be hiding. First things first—have you eaten?'

'I have. How about you? And what are you doing here anyway? Aren't you supposed to be on nights again?'

'I still am. I came in when I heard the news on the radio. Luckily I'm coming back after days off so I'm pretty fresh. I'm heading off for a few hours' sleep and then I'll come on about eleven. Rowena is going to stay back late for me.'

'Sounds wonderful,' Alice said enviously. 'Maisy kept me up most of last night. Cripes! The one thing I haven't done is check up on Maisy. I'm just going to make the quickest call in history and then I'm all yours.'

Maisy, of course, was fine. 'We've been watching it on the news,' Mavis said. 'Jeremy rang as soon as he got to work, frantically asking what bus you would be on.'

'Oh.' It had never even entered her head that Jeremy would have been concerned she might have been involved, but there hadn't exactly been much time for introspection. 'I took the tram, Mavis. Have you spoken to him since?'

'No, but I didn't really expect to unless, of course, he hadn't seen you. I'm sure he's too busy to ring his old mum for a gossip.'

Alice laughed. 'You're hardly that, Mavis. He has been

really busy. He's been great,' she added, not even bothering to keep the note of admiration out of her voice.

'Well, if you see him, make sure he eats something. An army marches on its stomach.'

'I will,' Alice assured her, though with the breakfast Mavis had served him she was sure Jeremy had enough in reserve to last the month out.

Replacing the receiver, she turned to a waiting Fi. 'I'm all yours now.'

The experience Alice gained during that on call was like a condensed version of her full three months and would stand her in good stead for years to come. With the more senior doctors unavailable and tied up in Theatre, Alice made more decisions and judgements that day and felt the weight of a doctor's responsibility more heavily than she ever had before. And yet, far from being fazed by it, she actually revelled in it—well, most of it.

Doing a post-op check on Kim Earl, Alice felt an overwhelming sadness as she looked at the bed cradle holding the sheets and blankets away from the newly fashioned stump. Kim was too out of it to understand what had happened in Theatre but her red-eyed parents sitting stunned by the bedside told the whole story.

'How is she doing, Doctor?'

Alice looked up from the charts. 'She's stable. Her observations have been good since she returned to the ward. I've just got her haemoglobin level back from the lab and it's still low, despite the transfusion in Theatre, so I'm going to order her a further two units of packed cells. Has she spoken at all?'

'Just a few words,' Bill replied. 'Sister Fi said she wouldn't make much sense for a few hours with all the morphine and everything.'

'That's right,' Alice agreed. 'She's had a lot of sedation.'

'She asked where Ted was.' Bill said, his voice suddenly bitter. 'I didn't know what to say.'

Alice looked around. 'Has he gone to the canteen?'

'The pub, more like. He couldn't get out quick enough when Mr Khan told us about her leg.'

'You don't know that, Bill,' Sheila interjected. 'He's upset. We all are. Anyway, there's not much he could do right now.'

But Bill wasn't going to be brushed off. 'He could be here,' he retorted smartly. 'He could be here for her, loving her—that would be enough. Isn't that what it's supposed to be about?' His voice was thick with tears, and Alice listened as this bearded, tattooed man spoke with empathy and passion. 'Sure, sometimes you can't change what's happened—we'd all like a magic wand to make the past disappear—but that's not going to happen. He should stand by her now when she needs him most. What's Kim got now?' And then he broke down, his wide shoulder slumping as he put his head in his hands and cried. Cried for his beautiful daughter, and what she had lost.

'She's got you,' Alice said gently. 'And from where I'm standing, that's going to be more than enough.'

CHAPTER TEN

BY TWO a.m. exhaustion was definitely starting to set in. Drug chart, IV charts, a pile of sticky notes attached to her worksheet—they all blurred in front of Alice's eyes. She ached to see Jeremy, longed to see how he was coping, how the day's events had taken their toll on him.

'A and E just rang up. There's going to be a debriefing at nine for all staff who were on in A and E—they'll do the wards after. Will you go?' Fi asked.

Alice nodded without looking up. 'I guess. Hopefully they'll put on a decent spread.'

'You cynic, you. Don't you think it helps?'

Alice signed off the drug sheet she had written up, leant back in her chair and swivelled to face Fi. 'I'm not sure. I don't know if I'm into all this dissecting things, analysing how we felt, how we reacted. Sometimes I think it can only make things worse. I'll be far more interested in the medical debriefing when Samuel Donovan goes over all the data and histories. There's something to be gained from analysing that, but as for the rest of it…'

'Maybe you're right,' Fi said, stifling a yawn. 'Dragging it all up doesn't change what happened. I guess you either cope with it or you don't.'

The call bell interrupted the rather deep conversation, and as Fi got up to answer it Alice carried on with her work. She hadn't been strictly truthful with Fi. The only debrief she was interested in was with Jeremy. Knowing how he'd coped, how he'd reacted—with him she knew she could have shown her feelings.

'How's it all going?'

His eyes left Kim for a moment and travelled over to hers. 'Did she now?' he said softly.

'I know I should be grateful, I know you've all saved my life, it's just… It was my *leg*. What am I going to be like? What's Ted going to think? He's never going to want me now.' She started to cry and Alice could hear the note of hysteria creeping in again.

'Of course he'll want you.'

'You haven't met him. He likes me to look good, and I like looking good—I'm a model for heaven's sake…' She glared at Jeremy as if he were responsible for all mankind. 'Would *you* want me? Be honest, would you still want me?'

It was the ranting of fear, of morphine and desperation, and Jeremy had absolutely no need to answer, no need to reduce this conversation to a personal level—he had never done so before. But Alice watched in stunned silence as his hand left Kim's arm and he held her hand. Pulling a chair over, he lowered himself slowly.

'Ah, now, that's a question. Well, put it this way—just over a year ago I'd have been out that door without a second glance. Hell, I've chucked girlfriends for having their hair too short.' Alice felt her breathing quicken. He had been so good—surely he wasn't going to mess it up now? 'And then, like you, I was involved in an accident. OK, I didn't lose my leg, but I just about lost my life. My brain was so swollen I was unconscious for three weeks. My left kidney was torn from the abdominal wall and had to be reattached, and my back was broken. I was the lucky one, but I tell you it didn't feel like it at the time. Lying in traction for three months, not knowing if I'd ever really walk again, having to be spoon-fed, learning to talk and walk and go to the bathroom all over again. But I did it, and so can you, because we are the lucky ones. And if you don't believe me, there's a mortuary full of kids and grown-ups tonight who I can only imagine would love to be in your shoes.'

'Or shoe.'

Alice had to stop herself from gasping out loud as she heard the attempt at a joke escape from Kim's pale lips.

'Kim, I was as vain as a man can be—probably a bit like your Ted. Looks mattered, money mattered, image mattered. Or so I thought. My accident served as a huge wake-up call and, although I never want to be there again, I'm glad it happened, and I can say that honestly. And with the right attitude maybe some day so can you. Stare at the ceiling for the next week, cry your eyes out and mourn what you've lost. You deserve that. Then get on with it. Pick yourself up, dust yourself off and get on with living— and while you're at it, decide who's coming on the journey with you. Because, let me tell you, with what you're about to go through you need the best, and if Ted's not up to the job then it's time to say goodbye.'

Kim's eyes were heavy now. The morphine was kicking in again. Her head lolled on the pillow. 'But you got there in the end? You're happy now?'

Hot tears were trickling down Alice's cheek. She hardly dared move to wipe them in case she broke the moment and, more pointedly, in case she didn't hear Jeremy's answer.

'Not yet,' he answered with a simple honesty that tore at Alice's heart. 'But I'm working on it, and at least I can sleep at night now.' Again he looked at Alice and gave a tiny smile. 'At least, most nights.'

Fi crept in, apologising for being so long. 'I got stuck with bed four. Here's the Valium.'

'It's all right, Fi,' Jeremy said, his voice a dry whisper. 'Looks like she's settled.'

'Good. Look, I'm sorry, Jeremy, Intensive Care just rang—they need you.'

I need you, Alice wanted to shout as he made his way out through the curtains, but he was already gone—and, anyway, she had left it too late. Suddenly it hit her with a certainty beyond question that she had let go of the best thing that had ever happened to her and Maisy.

Needing some fresh air and a moment to herself to take it all in, she headed outside to stand in the staff car park.

'Don't tell Dianne.'

Shocked that anyone else was out here, Alice swung around in time to see Josh hastily stubbing out a cigarette.

Alice managed a thin laugh. 'Have you got any left?' But her attempt at laughter caught in her throat and she started to cry in earnest. 'Oh, Josh, I've messed everything up.'

He was over in a flash. 'Hey, Alice, what are you talking about? There's nothing that can't be fixed.'

But she was inconsolable. 'We were so much in love. I know it could have worked but at the time I was so scared it just seemed so impossible.'

Josh's arms were comforting around her, like the big brother she had never had. 'I assume we're talking about our mutual boss, though technically that could also qualify as Linda. You're not about to give me a coronary, are you? I haven't got things that wrong?'

Thumping his chest as he held her, Alice laughed through her tears. 'Can't you be serious for once?'

'For you, Alice, yes.' And for once Josh was serious. Steadying her, he sat her down. Pulling a packet of cigarettes out of his pocket, he offered her one but she shook her head. 'Now, how about you tell me about it, and we'll see if there's anything that can be done?'

'I don't really know how it started,' Alice began. 'I knew all about him—his reputation, I mean—and I never even considered he'd like me. Well, not that way. But as the days went on, we just…well, you know. I had a confrontation with Marcus, Jeremy was there, it ended up in bed—not straight away,' she added hastily, glancing over to check Josh's reaction, but he stood there non-judgementally, puffing away. 'Then the pregnancy really took a dive. I know it wasn't his fault but I started to blame him. Then once Maisy came along…' she started to cry in earnest '…I just couldn't believe he could still want me. I was feeling pretty low, I can't really explain it, then Linda came to visit.'

'To brighten up your day.'

It was the first time Josh had interrupted.

'Josh, she didn't mean to hurt me. She told me about her friend.'

'Linda hasn't got any friends.'

'Are you going to listen?'

Josh threw his butt onto the ground and stepped on it, his jaw tensing as she continued. 'She was really nice. She didn't know everything that had gone on. She told me about her friend, another single parent, and how it had been for her. Up in front of the family law courts, trying to explain away her latest boyfriend and fighting for custody of her own child. Marcus is getting married to a kindergarten teacher, for heaven's sake. What chance would I have? Anyway, Linda let it slip—and it *was* an accident, Josh—that they weren't on call that night, although Jeremy had told me he was. I even rang the switchboard to confirm it. Linda said he was up to his old tricks, pulling everyone in sight, saying anything to get them into bed.'

'And you believed her?' Josh's voice was deadly quiet.

'She wasn't to know what had gone on.'

Josh stood up then, his eyes blazing. It was the first time ever Alice had seen him angry. 'Of course she knew. I told you never to trust her. She knew, Alice, we all knew.'

'But how?' she begged, utterly bewildered.

'Linda and I were walking to work the day you were

admitted with Maisy, and you and Jeremy were in his car. As for the mix-up with the on-call, Jeremy specifically swapped with Mr Taylor so he could be there for you on your first night home with Maisy. You know Switchboard only goes by the roster in front of them.'

'Then when she came to see me…' Suddenly the jigsaw was beginning to fall into place.

'She was fully prepared to do a hatchet job, and the state you were in unfortunately made it all too easy. Alice, you've been so down on yourself, so wrapped up in doing things right for Maisy, you've failed to see how good Jeremy really is. Don't you think you'd look better in the family courts—and it's doubtful that it will ever come to that—in a happy stable relationship with a guy who loves you and who's been through it all with you? And, as much as Linda goes on that Jeremy would sleep with anyone, she conveniently forgets she was someone he'd rejected.

'I never told you this, it never really seemed relevant. A few nights before Jeremy had his accident there was a surgeons' ball. Linda made a big play for him. I lied today—it was the second time I've seen her wearing lipstick. It was awful. She had too much to drink. I know Jeremy can be a bastard at times but he tried to let her down gently. She just wouldn't take the hint. It got really embarrassing. In the end he turned around and in that dry snobby voice he's perfected so well he said to her, ''Madam, please, control yourself.'' Everyone cracked up laughing, and in fairness to Jeremy it was entirely merited, but it was awful just the same. Linda turned to stone. She didn't see him again till the day he came back, the day you started.'

Alice raked her fingers through her limp hair. 'Oh, poor Linda, no wonder she hates me. It must have been awful for her, seeing that Jeremy fancied me.'

'He doesn't fancy you, Alice, he *loves* you. All that poor guy has ever done is love you. We've all got a past—me,

Jeremy, and even you. Hell, yours is two months old and sprouting teeth. We can't change our pasts but there's a hell of a lot we can all do about our future.'

She clutched her fists to her head, battling with the self-directed anger inside. 'What if I've left it too late?' she wailed. 'What can I say to him now, after the way I've been?'

'I'm sure you'll think of something. At the end of the day you could always resort to bit of honesty.' A glint appeared in Josh's eyes. 'But do us a favour, Alice, make it soon, for all our sakes. I'm starting to hope that I'm rostered for Theatre with Linda! It's enough to make a guy question his own sexuality.'

But 'soon' would have to wait. There were patients waiting, and later, as the sun rose and the curtains were drawn back on the wards for the six a.m. obs, Jeremy was called to Theatre and Alice was stuck on the wards. She didn't see him again until the ward round, her longing intensified as she saw the dark circles under his beautiful blue eyes, the dark blond stubble on his strong chin. That day would go down in history, Fi remarked, as the first ward round without Jeremy in a suit.

It would go down in history for other reasons as well. Arriving breathless at the apartment, Alice collided with Mavis on her way to the child health centre.

'You made it.'

'Only just. How has she been?'

Mavis gazed fondly down at the baby. 'She's been golden. You'd better take a brolly; the radio said there was a chance of rain.'

Alice looked up at the blue sky. 'They never get it right.'

'Got your gumboots all packed?' June asked as she weighed Maisy. 'I'll give you a letter to take to your new maternal and child health nurse.' She tutted a couple of times. 'Silly me, you won't have one of them where you're off to. I'd better address it to your new GP. Are you starting to get excited?' she asked, handing back Maisy.

'I'm not sure,' Alice mumbled, horrified at the thought of leaving for the country but not yet ready to burn her bridges.

June gave her a questioning look but didn't push. 'Well, we'd better fill in Maisy's progress book. You think you'll never forget the milestones, but by the time you've had a couple more it all starts to blur a bit.' She opened the yellow folder that contained Maisy's details—her length, her weight, her head circumference. Turning to the back, she started to ask Alice some questions.

'When did she start to follow your face with her eyes?'

Alice thought for a moment. 'After a couple of weeks.'

'Good.' June filled in the blank. 'How about her reaction to sound, a door banging perhaps or a hand clap. Does it startle Maisy?'

Alice nodded. 'Absolutely. There's rather a lot of door banging in the flat upstairs, unfortunately.'

'And how about her first smile?'

Alice gave a soft laugh. 'Well, Jeremy, my...' she hesitated '...my friend. He swears she smiled at him the day she was born, but I'd be more inclined to say since she was about four or five weeks old.'

June looked up from the book, pulling off her glasses, her bossy, no-nonsense exterior seeming to vanish for a moment. 'Then I'd say Jeremy's a lucky man. Their first smile is always something special, he was lucky to witness it. However, we'll write five weeks in the book, shall we?' Pulling on her glasses again, she picked up her pen.

It was a short, almost inconsequential conversation, but to Alice it was a revelation. Jeremy had sworn he'd seen Maisy's first smile, and there would be other firsts too that he would witness if only she would let him. Maisy and Jeremy had already shared so much. So he wasn't her biological father—he was the one who had been there when it had mattered, who had held her when she was born, showed her the moon and the stars.'

'Right, then, I'd better do this letter.'

Alice stood up, grabbing Maisy's nappy bag. 'June, there's somewhere I have to be. Look, could you hold off on the letter for now? I'll give you a call later in the week.' She paused. 'If I still need it.'

June gave her a wide smile. 'Or to make a further appointment. Good luck, Alice.'

Mavis had been right. Melbourne was known for its four seasons in one day. The blue sky had darkened and huge raindrops were starting to pelt from the dark grey sky, gaining in momentum. They would get drenched. About to turn back into the centre to ring for a taxi, she caught sight of a silver car. For a second her heart seemed to stop for there was Jeremy, waiting for her, ready to help her just as he always had been. Catching her eye, he ran out of the car. Throwing his coat over Maisy's carrycot, he ran with her the short distance to his car.

'Get in. I'll take care of Maisy.'

As she sat there in the warmth, watching as he diligently strapped her baby in, Alice realised that she wasn't really surprised to see him. After all, hadn't he always been there for them both when he was needed?

Slipping into the car beside her, he gave her a tired, cautious smile. 'Mum said you'd gone out without an umbrella, so I thought I'd better come when it started raining. He looked over at Maisy. 'How did she go?'

'She's put on another 300 grams.'

'That's good.' He looked utterly spent. He should have been in a bath, soaking away the pain and horrors of the last twenty-four hours, but instead he managed to turn and give Maisy a tender smile. 'You're catching up fast, aren't you, little lady?' As he reached forward to turn on the heater Alice's hand caught his.

'Thank you, Jeremy, for being there.'

'No problem. I didn't want her getting wet.'

'I mean for always being there, not just today.' She stared at her hand coiled tightly around his and she could feel his searching eyes questioning her movement, sense his uncertainty as to her sudden change. 'What would you say if I told you that saying goodbye to you was the biggest mistake of my life?'

For what seemed like an eternity he didn't answer, his eyes never for a second leaving her face. 'I'd be inclined to agree with you.'

'And what would you say if I told you I don't want to go to the country. I want to be here with you.' A sob escaped her lips as she finally admitted the truth.

'Hey, Alice.' He turned to face her. Gently disengaging is hand, he cupped her face with his palms. 'You don't have to stay here to have me. If you think things will be better for Maisy in the country then that's where we'll go.'

In stunned wonder she gazed at him through her tears. 'You'd do that for us? You'd give up your job?'

'In an instant. Alice, forget what I said about never living in a tent. If that's what it will take to keep you two, I'd pack up my backpack here and now. Admittedly I'd have to buy one first.'

She managed the tiniest laugh, then the tears came again. 'You don't have to leave your job. I only wanted to go to the country to give Maisy some security. I can't believe you'd do all this for me when I've been so awful, so doubting. How can you still love me?'

'Because I do, and that's all you need to know. Alice, you've had the most terrible time, you've been through so much. You were right to be doubtful—even I shudder at my past, and at the end of the day you had Maisy to think of. I know you had to be sure, and though I'm not going to deny it hurt I can understand it. You're a mother now, you had to put your child first—if anything I love you all the more for it.'

His lips met hers, his chin rough and unshaven scratching against her tears-soaked cheeks, his lips warm and full, quieting the sobs from her trembling mouth. And as Maisy drifted off to dream milky dreams he kissed Alice slowly and swore he'd never let her go again.

Finally, when the rain had stopped and the windows had long since misted over, he started the engine. Turning, he smiled, all traces of tiredness gone now. 'Where to, ladies?'

She glanced into the back, where Maisy slept on peacefully, and then her gaze drifted to Jeremy, the other love of her life, and Alice knew without a shadow of doubt that she was the luckiest woman alive. 'Take us home, Jeremy,' she said softly. 'Take us home.'

EPILOGUE

ALICE knew she should have been resting, but with the apartment to herself for once she had taken the opportunity of filling yet another photo album and making entries in Maisy's milestone book. Hearing the key in the lock, she let her eyes linger for a second longer on Maisy's adoption certificate, which certified Jeremy as her father. No matter how many times she gazed at the simple piece of paper, taking pride of place in Maisy's 'first year' book, it never failed to move her.

'Feeling better?' Jeremy asked as he staggered through the door, clutching a sleeping Maisy and the never-ending paraphernalia that seemed to accompany her.

'Much. I just needed a couple of hours. A and E was really busy last night.'

'Well, forget about work for now. Neither of us have to be back until Monday.'

He was right. The whole weekend lay before them and Alice stretched luxuriously on the bed. 'Was it a good party?'

Jeremy grinned. 'Well, not as wild as some I've been to, but it was certainly as noisy. Maisy had a ball. I'd better put her down, she's out of it.'

'How were the twins?' Alice asked as he returned. 'It's hard to believe that they're one already.'

'You'd better believe it. They're as cheeky and corrupt as their father. I caught Eamon stuffing ice-cream cake into poor little Maisy.'

Alice didn't believe him for a moment, knowing Jeremy was more than likely to have been the culprit there.

'Here, I got you a present.' He thrust a brown paper bag onto the bed. 'I'm becoming quite a celebrity at the local chemist. I think they officially class me as a ''sensitive guy'' now. How much more caring can you get—buying a pregnancy test kit with Maisy in a carry sling? I shall have to grow a beard and start eating lentils.' He was rambling now, unsure of her reaction.

So he'd noticed she'd missed her period! Opening the bag in silence, Alice finally found her voice. 'Actually, Jeremy, I beat you to it.' Padding through to the *en suite* bathroom, she handed him the indicator. 'I was going to tell you this evening.'

He didn't say anything for a moment, just stared at the tiny faint line which meant they were going to have another baby. 'We'll have two babies under two,' she said with a slight tremble in her voice. 'I'm going to get huge again.'

'Alice!' The rapture in Jeremy's voice said it all. 'Two babies will be wonderful, and Mum will always help out. And as for your size…as if that's going to worry me. You were huge when I met you!' Picking her up in his arms, he carried her the short distance to the bed. 'Now, young lady, it's back to bed with you. You should take the opportunity while Maisy's asleep.'

'But I'm not tired…' Alice protested.

Placing her gently down, he climbed on the bed beside her and kissed her slowly, deeply, leaving her in no doubt he was as delighted with the news as she was. 'That's good,' he said, coming up for air. 'Who said anything about sleeping?'

Modern Romance™
...seduction and
passion guaranteed

Tender Romance™
...love affairs that
last a lifetime

Sensual Romance™
...sassy, sexy and
seductive

Blaze
...sultry days and
steamy nights

Medical Romance™
...medical drama on
the pulse

Historical Romance™
...rich, vivid and
passionate

MILLS & BOON®

Winner at

2001 **IDEA** INTERNATIONAL
DESIGN
EFFECTIVENESS
AWARDS

MAT5

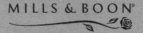

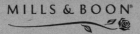

0702/73/MB38

Coming in July

❧

The Ultimate Betty Neels Collection

❧

✳ A stunning 12 book collection beautifully packaged for you to collect each month from bestselling author Betty Neels.

✳ Loved by millions of women around the world, this collection of heartwarming stories will be a joy to treasure forever.

Available at most branches of WH Smith, Tesco, Martins, Borders, Eason, Sainsbury's and most good paperback bookshops.

2 Books
and a surprise gift!

We would like to take this opportunity to thank you for reading this Mills & Boon® book by offering you the chance to take TWO more specially selected titles from the Medical Romance™ series absolutely FREE! We're also making this offer to introduce you to the benefits of the Reader Service™—

- ★ FREE home delivery
- ★ FREE gifts and competitions
- ★ FREE monthly Newsletter
- ★ Books available before they're in the shops
- ★ Exclusive Reader Service discount

Accepting these FREE books and gift places you under no obligation to buy; you may cancel at any time, even after receiving your free shipment. Simply complete your details below and return the entire page to the address below. *You don't even need a stamp!*

YES! Please send me 2 free Medical Romance books and a surprise gift. I understand that unless you hear from me, I will receive 4 superb new titles every month for just £2.55 each, postage and packing free. I am under no obligation to purchase any books and may cancel my subscription at any time. The free books and gift will be mine to keep in any case.

M2ZEB

Ms/Mrs/Miss/Mr ....Initials ....
BLOCK CAPITALS PLEASE

Surname ....

Address ....

....

....Postcode ....

Send this whole page to:
UK: The Reader Service, FREEPOST CN81, Croydon, CR9 3WZ
EIRE: The Reader Service, PO Box 4546, Kilcock, County Kildare (stamp required)